MW00716322

Ear-Witness

A Jessica March Mystery

For my family,
with special thanks to my daughter
Martha, who introduced me to
Parkdale and whose professional
advice and perceptive comments
have been invaluable.

Ear-Witness

A Jessica March Mystery

Mary Ann Scott

Boardwalk
Toronto • Oxford

RIVER WEST SCHOOL LIBRARY

© **Copyright 1996 Mary Ann Scott**

All rights reserved. No part of this publication may be reproduced, stored in a retrieval system, or transmitted in any form or by any means, electronic, mechanical, photocopying, recording, or otherwise (except brief passages for the purposes of review), without the prior permission of Boardwalk Books. Permission to photocopy should be requested from the Canadian Reprography Collective.

Boardwalk Books
A member of the Dundurn Group

Editor: Doris Cowan
Designer: Sebastian Vasile
Printer: Webcom

Canadian Cataloguing in Publication Data

Main entry under title:

Scott, Mary Ann, 1936–
      Ear-witness

"A Jessica March mystery".

ISBN 1-895681-12-X

I. Title

PS8587.C6318E27 1996   jC813'.54   C96–932109–0
PZ7.S36Ea 1996

Publication was assisted by the **Canada Council,** the **Book Publishing Industry Development Program** of the **Department of Canadian Heritage**, and the **Ontario Arts Council.**

Care has been taken to trace the ownership of copyright material used in this book. The author and the publisher welcome any information regarding references or credit for attribution in subsequent editions.

Printed and bound in Canada

Printed on recycled paper.

Boardwalk Books
2181 Queen Street East
Suite 301
Toronto, Ontario, Canada
M4E 1E5

Boardwalk Books
73 Lime Walk
Headington, Oxford
England
OX3 7AD

Boardwalk Books
250 Sonwil Drive
Buffalo, NY
U.S.A. 14225

CHAPTER 1

It was 7:35 A.M., and I was desperate. When I heard my mother coming up the stairs I took a dive for the couch and stuffed a pillow under my head. The door opened. My eyes shut.

"That's an inspiring sight," she said. "Bad night?"

I groaned, and pointed toward the floor, to the apartment beneath us. Blaming the noisy neighbours was a nice touch, I thought. But getting permission to cut school from an attendance fanatic like my mother would take more than nice touches.

I watched through half-closed eyes as she kicked off her shoes and collapsed into the chair across from me. She used to be easier to get along with when she came home tired after working all night, but the minute I turned fifteen she changed. Now she's tough all the time, especially about school. It's almost like she's waiting for me to do something brainless, like turn into a dropout or something.

"So what's the problem?" she said. "Tammi and Ray acting up again?"

I made a yes-sounding grunt. Our downstairs neighbours were OK most of the time, but occasionally, like last night, you'd swear they were bouncing off the walls.

Mom yawned. "Was it love or war this time?"

"War," I mumbled. I yawned too. "Ray and some other guy. There was a fight. Then Tammi bawled half the night. So did the baby."

Mom's mouth made a little "tsk" sound and she shook her head quickly from side to side. "Maybe you shouldn't babysit there any more. Maybe we should move."

"Yes!" I bolted to my feet. "What about one of those condos overlooking the lake. With a doorman!"

"Doorperson," she said. "Give me a break, Jess. They cost thousands a month! Thousands!"

"Just kidding." I hugged my arms across my chest and lifted my shoulders up to my ears. Then I glanced at the clock. If I was going to work up some sympathy, I had to get started. "Guess what I have to do today?"

"Not the book report," she said.

I nodded. I was miserable. I didn't hide it.

"Nervous?" she said.

"Nervous? Me, nervous? Petrified is more like it."

"Oh, Jess!" She looked pained. "You've worked so hard on it! You know it's good."

I rolled my eyes back into my head. "Yeah, sure," I said. "Who cares if I make an idiot of myself? It's a great report."

"But you only have to read it to the class!"

"The nightmare of all nightmares," I said. "And in case you hadn't noticed, I didn't sleep all night. I'm totally exhausted."

"Being overtired isn't a tragedy."

"Messing up because I'm so zonked isn't a tragedy? Getting a C when I deserve an A isn't a tragedy?" It was a good argument – top student forced to risk low grade because of unsympathetic parent. But she'd never buy it. Never.

She didn't. She shook her head, sort of sadly this time, like she was surprised I'd even bother with such a lousy excuse. I had one last hope. Sickness.

"What if I get galloping diarrhoea or something?" I put my hand on my gut. "I've already ..."

"Jess!" she said. "That's enough! Get dressed, and get going!"

Ms. Steely-Voice had spoken. I moved my butt.

Every piece of clothing I own makes me look like a blimp. My mother says I haven't lost my baby-fat yet, which is her way of saying I'm not really overweight at all. *Baby*-fat? At fifteen?

My green sweater wasn't too horrible, but it was the wrong length for my jeans. I tried on a skirt, then a different sweater, then some tights. Finally I decided on a black shirt, a vest, jeans and my boots. Then I fixed my hair. One of these days I'll do something different with it, like dye it red, or maybe black, or even cut it all off. Right now it's brown, shoulder-length, and boring. I might get rid of the bangs too. I lifted them with my comb and let them fall again.

They just brushed the tops of my eyebrows. Unexciting, but what else is new?

I was clumping down the stairs, just coming to Tammi and Ray's landing, when their door jerked open. Tammi poked her head out into the hall, then pulled back quickly when she saw it was me. She looked terrible; half-dead and wearing yesterday's makeup. Not her style at all. "Tammi?" I said. She shut the door slowly, as if she hadn't even seen me. I made a rude comment under my breath, and kept moving. Then I felt bad. She was probably in some kind of trouble again. Not nice, Jess. Not nice at all.

I was late, and cut across the neighbours' yard, passing two tall African women in long dresses and headscarves. Three small black-haired children, holding hands and chattering in a language I didn't recognize, crossed with me at the corner. A police car, lights flashing, turned down the street and stopped in front of our building. Two cops hurried inside. There weren't that many possibilities about where they were headed: our apartment; Tammi and Ray's; or the Orellanas' on the ground floor. I checked my watch, then turned and headed for school. I had enough on my mind. Other people's problems I couldn't handle.

Parkdale Collegiate is an old, red-brick building with turquoise doors and cement-block designs around the windows. It's set back from the street, surrounded by paved walkways, small grassy knolls, and trees. The picnic tables and park benches are a nice touch too, and so is the play equipment for the day-care kids. Nine hundred students, from all over the world, come here to get educated. Eight hundred and ninety-nine of them lost their baby-fat years ago.

English was the last period before lunch. Six of us were giving reports, and the fifth had just finished. I sat on the edge of my seat, waiting for the world to end. When Mr. Bronski called my name, I cracked my knee so hard on my desk that the red plastic Duo-Tang with my book report inside it fell to the floor and slid under the chair beside me. Evalita, my neighbour, retrieved it with long crimson fingernails and waved it in the air like she just won a prize. The class applauded.

I limped to the front of the room. My hands shook and my voice, when I got it working, sounded like a crow with strep throat. Thirty-eight faces stared. Thirty-five were glazed over with boredom, two were friendly, and one burned with hate. I blocked out everybody except Mr.

Bronski and Jon Bell, my fans. Jon is the smartest kid I know. He's probably even smarter than me. Tall and skinny, with a crest of white-blond hair, he looks like some rare, long-legged bird. When his nearly invisible eyebrows waved at me, I remembered to smile.

My book report was on a whodunit. I started out by talking about the main character, a woman detective who used her brains instead of her muscles to solve a crime. What I particularly liked, I said, was how she was smarter and more determined than the bad guys, smarter even than the police.

As part of my report I was supposed to talk about the type of book I was reviewing. So after I told them about the story, I went into this spiel about mysteries. I told them how the clues build up slowly, and how you have to read really carefully so you don't miss any of them. I even explained false clues, how mystery writers trick you into wondering if good people are bad, and bad people are good. I talked about endings, how they are both a surprise and not a surprise at all, because everything comes together and makes sense. I finished up by saying that if I had a choice between reading a scary book and seeing the same story made into a movie, I'd choose the book every time. (I'd actually see the movie too, but Mr. Bronski thinks we're all becoming illiterate TV and movie goons, so I left that part out.) The reason I enjoy reading best, I said, is because I like time to think about a story, to figure out the plot. On the screen, everything happens too quickly for that.

Mr. Bronski was pleased with me; his smile lit up the room. "Thank you, Jessica," he said. "An interesting presentation. Very interesting."

When he dismissed the class, I scooted out of there, fast. I was never fast enough, but I always tried.

"Hey, Fatso!"

I kept moving. Every time I said anything halfway intelligent in that class, this insect came after me. Ronny Roach had hated me for years. Running away didn't help, but what could I do? Stand around and wait to be insulted?

"You trying to get away from me, blubber-butt?" In the crush of bodies in the hall, he squirmed in beside me, then whipped a greasy-looking comb out of his back pocket and rearranged his stringy blond hair.

"An in-ter-rest-ing pre-sent-a-tion," he said. "Aren't we hot today! You like reading scary stuff, blubber-butt? Is that how fat girls get their kicks?"

8

I knew I had to do something about Ronny Roach and I knew I had to do it soon. To say he scares me isn't even close to the truth. He terrifies me. So far I hadn't let him see how much he got to me. Today I just managed to keep my cool; I didn't look up and I didn't talk. I just pasted a fake smile on my face and concentrated on getting away.

After a run-in with the Roach, even my locker looked good, almost like a friend. I grabbed my peanut butter and pickle sandwich and waited for Kelly, my buddy. To kill a little time, I rearranged the top shelf, hoping she'd show up while I was doing it. When she didn't, I took my lunch outside. The cafeteria was a zoo. There was no way I'd go there alone.

When I finished eating I checked out a few places Kelly might be, then went back to my locker for my books. I was fiddling with my combination lock when my name screeched out at me from somewhere near the ceiling.

"Jessica March, please report to the office immediately. Jessica March ..."

The message was repeated three times, while I stood there with my mouth open, inhaling the smell of old gym shoes. When I finally realized that it was the intercom I was hearing, and it was talking to me, I slammed the door shut, snapped the lock on and started running down the hall. For someone twenty pounds overweight, I'm in really good shape, but by the time I fell through the office door, my heart was bumping painfully in my chest and my imagination was killing me. Something horrible had happened to my mother: a car accident; a drive-by shooting; some terrible thing at the hospital where she worked...

The woman behind the counter was yakking on the phone. She refused to make eye contact, but I was in no mood to be ignored.

"I'm Jessica March," I said. "You called me on the intercom." Then I said it again, only louder.

She glared at me like I was ruining her day, and kept on yakking. Mrs. Carelli, the principal, beetled out of the inner office, and escorted me inside. A very large cop stood in front of her desk, looking out the window.

The principal pointed to a chair. "Sit down, Jessica. Thank you for coming so quickly."

If this morning was fear, *this* was terror. "What's wrong?" I gasped. "My mom?"

"Your mother is fine, Jessica, just fine." she said. "In fact I was just speaking to her on the telephone..."

Of course! Mom was at home today. Probably trying to sleep. Then I panicked. My mother. The principal. The cop. I groaned. I was afraid to ask, but I had to do it. "What have I done?" I said.

"Nothing, Jessica. Not a thing," Mrs. Carelli said. "You're here because the police need your help."

I took a deep breath, the first in what seemed like a long time. This was my first one-on-one conversation with this woman. I'd heard she was tough, but she seemed pretty decent to me.

She smiled. "I must apologize, Jessica," she said. "I didn't intend to frighten you. Why don't you sit down and relax, if you can, and Constable Bowes can explain."

I sat where she pointed, in one of the two chairs in front of her desk. The cop took the other. It creaked.

Mrs. Carelli introduced us. "Constable Bowes, Jessica March."

The cop looked at me and grinned. "The name's Sheena."

I slid my eyes to the front of her uniform. She was definitely a woman, a really big woman. Her hair, the colour Mom calls strawberry blond, was shorter than short, and she had a dimple in her chin.

She pulled out a small notebook, the kind with a little spiral across the top, and wrote down the date, and then my name.

"Jessica March," she said. "Age?" When she talked her words shot out of her mouth, like bullets.

"Uh, fifteen and a half," I said.

"You live at 582 Telborne Street, apartment three?"

"Uh-huh. Yes."

"Are you acquainted with the Bird family at that address? Mrs. Tammi Bird, Mr. Raymond Bird and a minor child, Brianna Bird, age four months?"

"Ray," I said. "He's called Ray."

"The baby?

"No, Mr. Bird."

She wrote that down. "You were employed by Mr. and Mrs. Bird for the purpose of babysitting Brianna Bird on Thursday evening from approximately 7:00 P.M. to approximately 10:00 P.M.?"

"That was last night," I said. "The baby was fine when I left. What's going on?"

She sat back, and examined me with bright blue eyes. "Mr. Bird was killed last night."

"Killed!" I said. "You mean he's dead? Ray's dead?"

She nodded.

"How? I mean, I saw him! He was alive at ..."

"Murdered," she said. "Some time during the night."

I leaned back in my chair. "Murdered!" I said. "I can't believe it. Murdered! How?"

Constable Bowes closed her notebook and slipped it into her shirt pocket. Her voice was softer now, more ordinary. "Maybe you'd come down to the station and give us a statement? We talked to your mom this morning. She said you often hear ... noises from their apartment?"

"Uh, sometimes," I said. What I usually heard was Tammi and Ray doing some pretty intimate stuff, like banging their bed against the wall, and making crazy animal sounds. Either that, or fighting like two tomcats. I looked at the principal. "Sure," I said. "If I can get off school."

Mrs. Carelli smiled. "No problem," she said. "Jessica won't have any difficulty catching up. She's a very good student."

A warm humming feeling zipped through my body, and I grinned all over my face. Mrs. Carelli smiled some more. So did Constable Bowes.

"This is really great for my reputation," I said. "Hauled off by a cop in the middle of the afternoon." I was sitting in the front passenger seat of the cruiser. When I looked back at the school, I didn't see anyone watching. Darn.

"I shoulda cuffed you," Sheena said. "Coulda staged a little tussle there in the hall. I can see the yearbook now. "Top Student Nabbed by Police in Office!""

My mouth twitched at one corner. "There's this guy hassling me," I said. "I wouldn't mind him knowing. If he thinks I'm tough, maybe he'll leave me alone."

"Somebody saw. A girl," she said. "She was sneaking a smoke behind the steps. It'll get around. Is this serious hassling or what?"

"He's not trying to touch me or anything. Just insults. Name-calling," I added.

"Such as?"

"Stuff about my body. Blubber butt. Thunder thighs. You know."

"Sexual harassment," she said. "Want me to talk to him? Make him wet his pants?"

I laughed. "Well, I might. I mean, I haven't decided what to do yet. He's been on my case for a long time, but he's never actually done anything, so ..."

"Any time, just give me the word. If you want him to think you're tough, tell him I charged you with assault. Assault with intent to wound. Because of that biker whose nose you broke." She hooted a great laugh and twinkled her eyes sideways.

I sat there, grinning from ear to ear, until I remembered why I was there. "What happened to Ray?" I asked.

"Wife wakes up in the morning, finds him dead."

"He was killed in the apartment? Right below me?" I could easily have freaked out over that. Very easily. Mom was at work all night, so I was alone, just one floor above a murder. I shivered. My back felt like somebody dropped an icicle down my shirt.

"How?" I whispered. "How did he die?"

"If I tell you that, I'll get in hot poop."

"I didn't hear a gun or anything."

Sheena moved one hand from the steering wheel, clutched an imaginary knife and plunged it into her chest. "I didn't tell you nothing," she said.

We rode the rest of the way in silence.

CHAPTER 2

At the police station, which was up near College Street, Sheena took me into a stuffy little interview room to meet Bud, the cop in charge of the murder investigation. He had to be over thirty, but with his bulging muscles and thousand-watt smile, he looked just like a Ken doll.

He pointed to where he wanted me to sit. "I'm the lucky guy who'll be asking the questions," he said. "Sheena here will take notes." Then he flashed his teeth and pulled up a chair. "So, Jessica ..."

Talking to Sheena was easy, but being in this place, with this man, made me nervous. Like, what are you supposed to say when a cop says So?

"Uh, it's Jess," I said. "Everywhere but school, I'm Jess."

"So, uh, Jess. You live in the same building as the Birds, right?"

"Right." I flashed some teeth too, just for practice.

"Where in relation to their apartment?"

"The next floor up. Right on top of them," I said.

"Who lives there? You, your parents? Anybody else? Sisters, brothers?"

I sat up straight in my chair. "Just me and my mom," I said.

"No dad?"

I stretched my legs out in front of me and admired my boots.

"Nope."

"So where is he?" Bud asked. There was something weird about his face but it took me a minute to figure out what it was. He was smiling, but only from the mouth down.

"Gone," I said. "I thought I was here to tell you stuff about the Birds."

"Just answer the question, please, Jessica."

Now he wasn't smiling at all. His mouth was a grim slit in the bottom of his face, and his voice had an edge to it, like Mom's does when she's really mad.

"He doesn't live with us. I already I told you that." This guy wasn't cute at all. He was mean-looking, with a personality to match.

"When did he leave, Jessica? Last year? Last month? Last week? Yesterday?"

He was really ticked off now, but I was pretty irritated myself, and I could sound just as rude. "He left when I was nine." I said.

Buddy-boy didn't miss a beat. "I guess your mom has a boyfriend, eh? Does he live with you? Nice-looking woman like that, I bet she's got men crawling all over her."

The man was a pig. I stared through him to Sheena, who was sitting just behind him, but off to one side, where he couldn't see her without turning around. She made a pistol with her fingers and pointed it at Bud's head.

"Just Mom and me," I said, as sweetly as I could. "Didn't I tell you that already?" I wasn't really lying, not much. Enough to cause a heap of trouble, but I didn't know that yet.

"Tell me about the Birds," he said, all charm again. "How well do you know them?"

"Pretty well. I look after the baby two or three times a week. Sometimes I talk to Tammi."

"And Mr. Bird?"

"He's OK, I guess. Was OK."

"You didn't like him?"

I couldn't stand him. Ray had sneaky eyes, and he was bad-tempered and sarcastic, but I didn't want to cut up somebody who was dead. "We hardly ever talked," I said. "Except when he paid me."

"And you babysat last night?"

"Yeah."

"From when to when? Be as exact as you can."

"I went downstairs at quarter to seven and came back up at about ten-fifteen."

Even when he was asking questions, Bud was staring at the ceiling, like he couldn't stand the way I looked, or I was boring him silly. "Were both Mr. and Mrs. Bird there at quarter to seven?"

"Yeah."

"Where were they going?"

"Tammi went to bingo. I guess Ray went to work."

"Where's that?"

"Some bar on Queen Street. I don't know the name of it, but I don't think it's a very nice place. My mom says it's a sleaze joint."

He nodded. His eyes were closed now. "They come home together?"

"No, they never do, never did. Ray worked late. Tammi came home, then I left."

"I understand from your mother that you were alone last night, while she was working. Right?"

Now he was drumming his fingers on his leg, like he'd rather be somewhere else. I could relate to that.

"Right," I said.

"Where does she work?"

"Queen Street Mental Health Centre. She's a nurse."

He looked a little bit interested at that. Well, maybe not interested exactly, but his mouth sort of flattened out when I said it.

"Did you see or hear anything unusual last night?" he asked.

"Well, I hear fighting all the time, but ..."

Suddenly I had his full attention. His eyes bored into mine, like we were in some sort of staring contest. "Physical stuff or just words?" he said.

"Both, I guess. Last night was different, though. It was two guys. There was a lot of yelling, and then somebody fell down, or fell into the wall or something."

"Did you recognize any voices?"

"Well, one was Ray, that's for sure. I hear him, uh, *heard* him all the time. Roaring all over the place. I don't know who the other one was."

"Could you hear what they said? Think carefully now, Jess, this could be extremely important."

I thought as hard as I could, but nothing came. "They woke me up," I said. "Several times, I guess. But I didn't hear words, just, you know, loud voices." I paused, because I was still trying to remember. "For some reason, I think they were fighting about money. I don't know why I think that."

"Could there have been more than two people?"

"Tammi was there too. And the baby," I added.

"What time was this?"

I shrugged. "Once was just after two. That's probably the only time I checked the clock."

"Did you hear anything else? Other than two men arguing and someone falling down?"

"After that, I heard Tammi. She was crying for a really long time. Sort of talking and crying, crying and talking." This eye contact stuff was killing me, but if I didn't do it, or at least try to do it, I was afraid he'd think I was lying.

"Any idea who she was talking to?"

I shrugged again. "Sorry," I said.

"You didn't hear anything or couldn't tell who it was?"

"I didn't hear. Maybe she was talking to herself. Or to the baby."

He nodded. "You said you heard fighting all the time. What kind of fighting?"

"Just ... Tammi and Ray. That's the way they were."

"You need to be more explicit than that, Jessica. Tell me what you heard."

"Mostly words, yelling. Once I saw her with a black eye." I paused. "He was pretty mean, even in front of me."

"Can you give me an example?"

This was really hard work, and I didn't like it. Snitching isn't my style. I tried looking at the ceiling too, but it didn't have any answers. And Bud was waiting, drumming those fingers. I sighed. "Ray would say stuff like *Shut your bloody trap* or *I'll shut it for you*. Or, I don't know, make fun of her, like he knew everything, and she knew nothing. He was always telling her how stupid she was."

"What a creep," Sheena said.

Bud flashed his eyes at her. The message they sent was unmistakable. It was *shut up*. He turned to me.

"Did Mrs. Bird ever say anything to you about their relationship?"

I thought about that. "Once she did. We were out on the back stairs, it must have been last fall, because she was already looking really pregnant. We were just sitting there in the sun when all of a sudden she starts crying. Then she said that Ray used to be really nice to her, but when she got big, with the baby, he changed."

Sheena looked directly at me, shook her head and pointed her thumb towards the floor.

"Anything else you can tell us?" Bud said. "Anything you saw or heard that seems unusual?"

I thought some more. "There's the money," I said. "Ray always has ... had, a whole lot of money."

"How much is a lot? A couple of hundred?"

Did this guy think I was a kid or what? "More than that," I explained. "He had this big wad with a gold dollar-sign clip on it. Hundreds and fifties. Lots of them. Like maybe thirty hundreds, and at least that many fifties. He always had money like that. Once he showed me a thousand dollar bill."

Bud glanced quickly at Sheena, who bent her mouth down at both ends, and nodded.

"The Birds have many visitors?" he said.

"Nope."

"People dropping around? Coming to the door?"

"No." I knew what he was thinking, that Ray was a drug dealer. If he was, he didn't do it from home.

"Ever smell grass there, or hash?"

"No. Never."

"You know what they smell like?"

"Yeah."

"Nice girl like you knows that?"

"You'd have to be pretty dumb to be in high school and not know that," I said. "Not that I ever..."

"Ever see any white powder lying around?"

I shook my head.

"OK, Jess. Thanks," he said. "This has been very helpful. Uh, sorry if I made you mad earlier. Guess you don't like talking about your old man, eh?" He flashed his fake smile.

I smiled too, but just a little, to make him think I had no hard feelings.

"Sheena here will type up your statement, so you can sign it," he said.

Sheena's mouth moved sideways on her face. "Just give *Sheena-here* a few minutes, then she'll drive you home."

Toronto is an enormous city. The very rich live in mansions on quiet streets, or in elegant condominiums overlooking the lake. The less rich own single-family homes with one or two cars in the driveway. The rest of us rent; houses, townhouses, apartments, whatever we can afford. Mom and I live on the top floor of a hundred-year-old triplex. Our car, a ten-year-old clunker, gets parked on the street.

When Sheena and I rolled down Telrose Avenue in the big cruiser, three other cop cars and a police van were pulled up on the sidewalk in front of a No Parking sign. Small groups of neighbours stood around in clusters, chatting and watching the show. Ronny Roach and two of his buddies were among them, sharing what was probably a cigarette. For the second time that day I was aware of unfriendly eyes.

"See ya," Sheena said. She watched me get out and start across the street. Then she took off towards the only cruiser with someone still in it. A guy in a uniform sat in the driver's seat with the door open. When he saw her coming, he swung his legs to the ground and stood up and stretched, like he'd been sitting a long time. A police radio crackled with static. Somebody turned it off. The silence was deafening.

Mom, Mrs. Orellana, and the Orellana kids were hanging out on the porch. The grassy area in front, which Mom laughingly called *the lawn*, was surrounded by waist-high yellow tape. Inside the roped-off area, two cops were crawling around on their knees, saving bits of garbage in small plastic bags.

I perched on the steps just below Mom. I hadn't seen her since I left for school, but it seemed like a week. I had this overwhelming urge to throw my arms around her neck, but I didn't. "Where's Tammi?" I said.

"Gone to her friend's place." Mom rubbed my shoulders for a second. I leaned back on her legs. It's spooky sometimes, how we almost read each other's minds.

"Why aren't you sleeping?" I asked. Then I looked around at all the activity going on. "Too noisy?"

"I don't have to work tonight," she said. "I traded shifts. Jess, you know Mrs. Orellana. And Flavia, and Carlos."

We all smiled. The Orellanas were new. They'd been living in the ground floor apartment, the one underneath the Birds, for about three weeks now. Even though the kids are more or less my age, we hadn't said more than Hi. They're refugees, from some place in Central America. I felt shy around them for some reason, and although they spoke really good English, I never knew what to say. Usually when you meet new kids you can ask them stuff about where they were before, like what school they were at, or what city they lived in. But when people have had to leave their country, I figured they might not want to talk about it. And maybe they'd think I was ignorant if I asked.

The girl, Flavia, had awesome olive skin and long straight hair tucked behind her ears. She looked older up close; she could easily be seventeen. Carlos was probably about my age. He was chunky, with big muscular shoulders and arms. His hair, pulled back into an elastic, was long too. Mrs. Orellana was an older version of Flavia. She and Mom looked kind of nice, sitting there side by side. Both skinny, with their dark hair done up in a knot. Both really attractive women.

"What did the police want?" Mom asked.

I looked into her eyes. "I guess I heard the murder happen," I said. "They wanted me to tell them everything, stuff I didn't even know." Then I turned to Flavia. "Did you hear anything?"

Her eyes swung to the police all around us, then she looked at her mother and said something in Spanish. Mrs. Orellana shook her head. "No," Flavia said.

Sheena came up the walk and I introduced her to everybody. She nodded, touched me on the head, and went inside.

"Is he still in there?" I said. "Ray?" I hadn't wanted to ask, but I had to know.

"No," Mom said. "They took the body away around noon. How was your book report?"

The body. I've never seen anybody dead, and that's just fine with me. I looked down at the step I was sitting on, and imagined Ray climbing it last night. A one-way trip. Unless you count being carried out.

"The book report, Jess. How was it? Did you survive?"

"Yeah, sure." I said. "It was a piece of cake."

Flavia and Carlos looked at me and frowned.

"What's going on?" I asked. "Did I say something stupid?"

"No," Mom said. Then she laughed. "But a book report isn't really a piece of cake."

"You know what I mean," I said.

"But the Orellanas don't."

Flavia said something to Carlos in Spanish, then turned to me. "Sayings like that are very difficult when you do not grow up with the English," she said. "A piece of cake, what does that mean? Used the way you said it."

I started to explain. "I had to read a book report in front of the class this morning," I said, "and I had my underwear in a knot about it..."

They laughed, and so did Mom, but I didn't get the feeling they were being mean. Carlos whispered something to Flavia, who elbowed him sharply in the ribs. "Animal!" she said. "Men are such animals!" She turned back to him. "I will tie yours in a knot if you do," she said.

"I did it again, didn't I?" I said. "Underwear in a knot. That means I was very stressed out. You know stressed?"

Flavia nodded. "Piece of cake?" she said.

I turned to Mom for help. She looked up at the sky. "Piece of cake." She thought for a moment. "You say that when something's easy and pleasant to do. Like eating cake."

We all looked at the sky now. It was deep blue and cloudless. Sheena came out and sat with us. She looked up too. "Nice," she said.

If Mom hadn't been with me, I would *never* have gone back inside that door and up those stairs. The worst part was passing Tammi and Ray's apartment. I couldn't stop thinking that there was still something horrible in there: the murderer, maybe; or the dead body, even though I knew both were gone. Well, I knew the body was gone because Mom told me it was. And the murderer had to be gone, because if he was still there, the cops would have caught him. Unless he came back later, to revisit the scene of the crime, like some murderers are supposed to do.

Ray could have come back too, if he turned into a ghost. Fortunately I stopped believing in stuff like that years ago. Even when I was alone in the middle of the night, and the wind was howling and the whole building creaked, I was still pretty sure there weren't any. Almost sure.

CHAPTER 3

After dinner (spaghetti and home-made vegetarian tomato sauce, my specialty) the three of us: Mom, me, and Raffi, Mom's boyfriend, were sitting around in our big front room telling lies.

My lie was hiding how scared I was. If Ray could get murdered, we could get murdered too. Maybe Mom knew how I felt, and maybe she didn't, but I wasn't giving anything away.

Mom and Raffi were carrying on as if having somebody killed in the apartment right under us happened every day, like it was nothing. This was for my benefit, of course, so I wouldn't get in a big flap. The big flap I was already in, which they didn't know about. Maybe.

They were both really worried too. I could tell, because the things they were saying were so totally fake. For instance, Raffi said Ray must have been killed because of some private dispute, so we didn't have anything to worry about. I wish! How did anybody know what kind of dispute it was? There could be a serial murderer on the loose for all we knew. The thing Mom kept harping on about was how Tammi wasn't killed too. No kidding! That makes the rest of us safe? I didn't believe anything either one of them said. The funny thing was, I don't think they believed what they were saying either.

Mom was sitting on the couch, drinking a little cup of strong coffee. Raffi was clearing up the dishes. I was still at the table, but I'd pushed my chair back and turned it so I could see them both. The reason I could do that is because we have one of those all-purpose rooms, with the kitchen along the back, the dining room in the middle and the living room up front, by the window. Because we're on the top floor, the ceiling slants down to meet the walls, which makes us feel sort of cozy, unless its summer, when the whole place turns into an oven.

It's a nice room, and since it's only May, it's pretty comfortable. The furniture is all old, but it's painted and slip-covered so everything is either wood or a soft buttery cream colour, to match the walls and the rug. A huge painting of me, wearing my bright red sweater, hangs over the couch. Raffi painted it, as a surprise, for Mom's birthday. I love it. It makes me look at least seventeen.

Pretending I'm not scared, if it's a lie at all, is harmless. Mom's and Raffi's lies, letting on there's nothing to be scared of, are pretty harmless too. But there was another lie on my conscience, one I had to think about. I hadn't been exactly honest with that cop when he asked if Mom had a boyfriend. Now I had to decide whether to tell Mom and Raffi what I'd said, or just keep my mouth buttoned and hope no one would find out.

The last time I took the button-up option, I'd been grounded for a month. I was only twelve then, and still thought I was smarter than my mother. Kelly and I'd been fooling around with makeup samples in a drug store when all of a sudden she turned her back to the overhead camera and slipped a shiny new lipstick into the pocket of her jeans. Revlon. Some purple colour.

She was caught, mostly because I lost my cool and started hissing at her, telling her what a stupid ninny she was and ordering her to put it back. Kelly was in big trouble. She didn't exactly blame me for it, but she was a little chilly for a while. I hadn't taken the lipstick, and I hadn't helped Kelly take it either, so my problem wasn't because of the shoplifting. It was because I pretended the whole thing didn't happen. When the cop came to the front door to talk to Mom, to let her know about the riff-raff I was hanging out with, I left by the back. That was the worst thing I could have done. I wasn't just grounded, I was grounded with housework: washing walls, and curtains, and rugs, and bedspreads; cleaning out closets and cupboards. Nobody needs to be that clean.

Pretending something didn't happen doesn't work, so I had to tell the truth about what I said to the cop. But how?

One way to confess something is to build up to it slowly. You act all quiet and depressed for a while. Then, when you've got everybody all worried you're getting some terrible disease, you cry a little, and eventually burble everything out. But you've got all this sympathy first.

Sometimes I think my mother must have taken a course about teenagers or read a book about us, because things I used to do, all my life, that worked just fine, have been bombing out like you wouldn't believe. Now she's into this dumb theory about not rewarding negative behaviour, so if I try acting depressed, she ignores me, or says something charming like *Spit it out, Jess!*

So that's what I decided to do. I'd just tell her, straight out, quick and dirty.

"I lied to the cops," I said. "Sort of lied, anyway."

Mom's posture changed from rag-doll to stiff-as-a-board within micro-seconds. "What?" she said. "What? Why on earth would you do that?"

"You had to be there," I said. "This jerk cop asked if you had a boyfriend. But the way he said it sounded like he thought you were some kind of tramp, so I got mad. Then he asked if you had some guy living here. Only what he did was ask both questions at once. So when I answered the one about somebody living here, it was like I was answering both. *Just Mom and me,* I said.

"Was that woman cop there?"

"Yeah, but it was a guy who asked the questions." I didn't mention the interrogation I got about my father because my mother's least favourite person in the whole world is Gordon March. It never seems to occur to her that if it wasn't for him, she wouldn't have me. And if it wasn't for me, she wouldn't have a big fat child-support cheque every month either.

My mother has such a hate-fix on my father that I decided to stop seeing him until she cooled off. That was three years ago. But I blame my dad too. He could have made things better. If he cared. If he wanted to see me.

Raffi stood up and stretched. "So the cops don't even know I exist?" he said. "They don't know your mom is seeing anybody?"

"You got it."

"I'd be lying if I said I wasn't scared of them. Me and every other black guy in Toronto. I need the police sniffing around me like I need a hole in my head."

Mom's voice was shaky. "Don't even joke about that," she said. One of Raffi's friends, who is also black, was recently shot at by the cops for no reason at all.

Raffi hardly ever got upset, so when he did, you really noticed. "Derek is still in the hospital," he said. "For nothing. For being in the wrong place at the wrong time."

"He shouldn't have run, though," Mom said. "I'm not saying what the cops did was OK, but you have to remember, if they say halt, you halt."

Mom really likes Raffi a lot. He's been her boyfriend since I was eleven, but he doesn't live with us. He has a tiny apartment across the street. So I didn't lie, not really.

CHAPTER 4

It was Saturday morning, the second day after the murder, and I was just about awake when Kelly phoned. "Where were you?" I asked. "I looked all over the school for you!"

"I messed up," she said. "I'll tell you later. Can I come over?"

"Now? Sure. Just don't panic when you see the yellow crime-scene tape. Ray Bird was murdered yesterday."

"Jeez, Jess, that's, that's ...awful. The big guy married to that airhead with the hair?"

"Yeah. Well, Tammi is a bit of an airhead, I guess, but I feel sorry for her." I yawned. "Are you coming right now?"

"Can I?" she whispered into the phone. "The Pain is watching TV. If I don't get out of here while she's distracted, I'm going to have her trailing after me all day."

The Pain is Kelly's little sister. "Come now," I said. "Please."

Kelly weighs almost as much as I do, but she's a little taller, a natural blonde, and absolutely beautiful. We've been best friends since kindergarten. Lately though, since she's been going out with Joey, I've been feeling kind of pushed away. Once I tried to talk to her about it, but all she said was that having a boyfriend changed her life, and I couldn't understand until I had one too. Sometimes I wish she wasn't so pretty, but I guess that's mean.

After I got dressed, I watched for her from the front window. When I saw her trudging around the corner I raced downstairs and held the door open, so she wouldn't push the buzzer. "The Countess is still asleep," I said.

When we got back upstairs, Mom was standing at the door, making a liar out of me. "I am not," she said. "Although I might be if some dummy hadn't phoned at the crack of dawn."

"Oh-oh," Kelly said. "That was no dummy, that was me. I waited 'till nine-fifteen..."

"Not to worry," Mom said. "It's time I was up anyway. Have you had breakfast? Jess might make French toast if we ask her nicely." She leaned her head on my shoulder. "Please, Jess, please." This was exactly what I used to do to her. *Please, Mom, please,* I'd whine. It was one of those things that used to work.

"Sounds great," Kelly said. "I'll help."

Mom wandered back down the hall. "Save me some," she called. "I'm going to have a shower."

I took eggs and butter out of the fridge, and bread and maple syrup from the cupboard. Kelly leaned against the wall, watching, while I told her about the murder. After she heard the basics, she started asking questions.

"If Tammi was in the apartment when Ray was killed she must have seen the murderer, right?"

"Right," I said. "I guess." I cracked the eggs into a bowl, and messed them around with a fork. Then I added milk and some nutmeg.

"So why didn't he kill her too?"

"Maybe he wasn't mad at her," I said.

"Jess! She can identify him!"

I turned the gas on under the frying pan, threw in a hunk of butter and watched it sizzle. "Yeah," I said. "She could do one of those drawings. Pick eyes and noses and join them together."

"How many noses does he need?" Kel asked.

"Ha ha," I said. "Maybe she was in the back bedroom and he didn't even know she was there."

"But wouldn't she come out when she heard all that noise?"

"I don't know. Maybe not, if she was scared." I soaked six slices of bread in the egg mixture, and put three of them in the pan to fry.

"And why didn't she call the cops?"

"When they were fighting?" I asked.

Kelly nodded.

"Maybe she didn't expect the guy to have a knife, " I said. "Here, you can set the table."

"What about after, when Ray's dead?" She took the knives and forks from me and stood there, holding them.

"Well, we don't know exactly when that happened."

"Look, you're the one who said you heard somebody falling in the night..."

"Yeah," I said. "I think he was killed then. And that's when she started bawling." I took the cutlery from her hand, and set three places. Kelly didn't even notice.

Mom, all pink and shiny from her shower, opened the fridge door and peered inside. "I don't know what I want," she said.

I poured three glasses of orange juice and handed her one.

"Do we know when she called the cops?" Kelly asked.

"They came just after Jess left for school," Mom said. "Tammi said she just woke up and found him dead. Right then. In the morning."

"Even though she cried all night?" I asked. "She's lying!"

"Maybe she was in shock," Mom said. "Maybe she couldn't function at all."

"And maybe," Kelly said, "she was waiting for him to die."

Kelly has always had an absolutely wicked imagination, but this was too much. Mom and I stared at her.

"That's a horrid thing to think about," Mom said. "I can't believe Tammi would do that."

"Why not?" Kelly said. "If she hated him? If she had enough of being bashed around? Maybe she just sat there and let him bleed to death."

"You're sick, Kel," I said. "I don't think so. Tammi isn't the smartest person I ever met, but she's not mean. And she was really upset that morning. At least I thought so." I looked at Mom. "What do you think?"

"She was really upset," Mom said. "But that could be for any number of reasons. Watch the toast, Jess."

I flipped three perfect pieces onto a platter, which I put on the table. Then I carefully laid the last three in the pan.

"How else can we explain why she didn't get help until morning?" Kelly asked.

"We can't," I said. "Let's eat."

After breakfast we left Mom with the dishes and walked over towards the library, so I could return my book-report book and take out another. There was a tournament going on at the tennis courts beside the school, and we sat on a bench to watch. The players were all men.

"So what's happening with you?" I asked. "Where were you yesterday?"

Kelly's eyes followed the game in front of us as the ball flew from one end of the court to the other. "I did a dumb thing," she said. "I went to that clinic, the place where you can get birth control stuff." Then she turned towards me and made a goofy face.

I was quiet for a minute. I wasn't exactly shocked, but I wasn't exactly expecting something like that either. "So what happened?" I said.

She sighed. "I never even talked to anyone. I just sat in the waiting room for a while, and then I took off."

"You could go back," I said. "You want me to go with you?"

"I don't know. Thanks, though."

An old man with a small rat-like dog on a retractable leash sat on the bench beside us. "Where are all the women?" Kelly said. "Don't they play tennis?"

"Home with the babies," I said.

She shrugged, looked sideways at the old man, and nudged me to my feet. We followed the path that ran beside the school and came out onto Jameson. "I came this close," she said, showing me a space the width of her thumb, "to letting Joey do it. Without ... anything."

"Oh, Kel," I said. "Aren't you scared that ..."

She shook her head and turned a bright pink. "It's not that easy to stop him, Jess. And anyway," she blushed, "I really want to do it."

"This is probably a dumb question," I said. "But why? Why no condom?" This was something I couldn't figure out at all. Why everybody didn't use them, like you're supposed to.

She giggled. "You have to be there. Joey says it's like washing your feet with your socks on."

I didn't know what to say, then. It sounded to me like Joey wasn't thinking of Kelly at all, but who was I? I thought for a minute, then I decided. I was her best friend, that's who I was. Jealous, maybe, that she had a boyfriend and I didn't, but I didn't want her to get hurt.

"Doesn't he care about you?" I said. "What if he's got AIDS or something? What if you get pregnant?"

Kel looked up and down the street, like she was expecting to see somebody she knew. "He cares, and he doesn't have AIDS, and I won't get pregnant. He's just stubborn." Then she grabbed my arm and pulled me into the library.

It was obviously time to talk about something else. "I had another scene with the Roach," I said. "Yesterday. That's why I was looking for you."

"He's a slime, Jess. You're going to have to do something about him. I still think you should let Joey and the guys talk to him. Or whatever. Shake him up a little."

"Um," I said. Joey, Kelly's boyfriend, was huge, with arms and legs as big as trees. I didn't know whether I liked him or not, or even if I wanted to like him, but I knew exactly what I thought of his friends. I couldn't stand them. Guys who pass around joints on street corners and elbow each other when girls pass by aren't my kind of people. They might scare off Ronny Roach, but they scared me off too. I didn't want anything to do with them. It was time to change the subject again.

"Remember Mrs. Jones, in grade seven?" I said.

"Mrs. Jones and the erogenous zones!"

"Mrs. Zones, we called her. Do those, um, places really feel nice? When Joey does... whatever?"

Kel bit her bottom lip and crinkled up her eyes. "Yeah," she said. "If he's gentle, they feel totally superb."

"I can just see you," I said. "Making those little whimpering noises and heaving your butt up and down. Like in the movies."

Suddenly we were ten years old again, doubled over on a street corner, laughing so hard we almost peed ourselves.

CHAPTER 5

"Two double chocolate, one regular coffee," Sheena said. "Jess?"

I ordered a muffin and a tea. It was Monday, after school, a week and three days since the murder. The doughnut shop was crowded and full of second-hand smoke. My eyes stung, and after three minutes in the place I already stunk like an old ashtray. Sheena didn't seem bothered at all.

"Shoulda ordered something chocolate, Jess," she said. "Makes you grow. Look at me if you don't believe it."

"Is it a problem?" I asked. "Being so tall? Is that a rude question?"

"Nah. It was me who mentioned it first. It used to bother me. I was the biggest girl in the whole darned town when I was growing up. Now, on the force, being big is an advantage." She grinned, then took a huge bite from her first doughnut.

I peeled the paper off my muffin. "My problem is weight," I said. Then I put the muffin back on the plate.

Sheena frowned. "Nothing wrong with you. Still got a little baby-fat maybe. That's all."

"Nothing wrong that losing twenty pounds won't fix," I said. I looked down at the muffin. Blueberry, my favourite.

"Ah," she said. "Now I get it." She took another bite. Crumbs dribbled down her chin and settled on the dark front of her uniform. "You think about your body all the time, right? First thing the world sees about you, is that twenty pounds?"

"Maybe."

"You want to be some anorexic model?"

"Well I don't want to be anorexic, just thin."

"Hate your body?"

I groaned. How do you tell a cop to lay off?

"Think you look like a sack of potatoes with a string around the middle?"

"A walrus," I said. "In tight jeans." I had to work on my face. What she was saying was sort of funny, but she was making me feel stupid, and if it killed me, I wasn't going to laugh.

"Helps a lot, doesn't it? Being so down on yourself?" She demolished her second doughnut, then wiped her chin with the paper napkin.

I dipped the tea bag in and out of my cup, then sipped the contents. There aren't any calories in tea.

Sheena leaned across the table and looked me straight in the eyes. "There comes a point when you gotta decide, Jess. Get on with life, or dig a hole and bury yourself. I don't figure you for a hole-digger, but maybe I'm wrong."

I looked right back at her. "You have crumbs on your uniform," I said.

"Thanks." She brushed them off quickly, then pulled out her notebook. "Now," she said. "We got business to discuss. You said the Birds didn't have visitors. Could you be wrong? Mrs. Bird, says they had people there all the time. Mr. Bird did, late at night. And that's why she didn't pay any attention to their guest. Never even saw him, she says."

I closed my eyes. Tammi had to be lying, but why couldn't somebody else be the one to rat on her? Why me? When I opened my eyes again, Sheena was still there, waiting.

"This is a murder investigation, Jess," she said. "Loyalty to friends has no place here."

I shrugged to give myself a little time. "The only person I ever saw there was Tammi's girlfriend. The one who drives her home from bingo. Terri."

Sheena flipped back a few pages. "Theresa Goodwin," she said. "Real shapely brunette? Enough hair for three people?"

"That's her."

"I'm more interested in visitors for Mr. Bird. Late at night."

I knew I had to tell the truth, but I wasn't happy about it. "I don't think so," I said. "They'd have had to whisper all the time. Ray's voice was really loud; you could hear him all over the building. The door buzzer's loud too. Mom says it would wake the dead."

Sheena nodded, then wrote something down. "O.K.," she said. "Another thing. You talk to the Orellana kids at all?"

"We've walked to school together a few times. I like Flavia a lot."

"What about the guy, Carlos?"

I giggled. "He's strange. He's always telling us how many kilos he can lift, and how far he can run, and how many girls are crazy about him." I caught myself picking bits off the crusty edge of the muffin, where the round part juts out over the bottom, so I tucked it all up nicely in a napkin and stuffed it in an empty cup on the table beside us. It wasn't even very good, it was just there.

"Carlos just wants you to like him," Sheena said. "The whole family is up-tight. I tried to question them about what they heard the night of the murder." She rolled her eyeballs up into her head. "It was a total waste of time. Their dad wasn't even there, or so he said. Works half the night. At two jobs. Mom and the two kids were there all right but they're like the three monkeys. You know: *See no evil*; *Hear no evil*; and *Speak no evil*. It doesn't make a lot of sense to me that you'd hear all that yelling and none of them heard a darn thing."

"Maybe they're all heavy sleepers," I said.

"More likely they're scared to talk to cops. Where they come from, police aren't the nice guys we got in Canada, you know."

I thought about Raffi's friend, and what happened to him, but it didn't seem to be a good time to mention it.

"I was wondering if the kids would talk to you," she said. "Assuming everything is on the up-and-up, and they aren't hiding anything. If you're real cool about it, and don't put any pressure on? I'm sure they know something. I can feel it in my gut."

"I could try, I guess," I said.

What else could I say? I didn't want to be a snitch, but if I said that, she'd probably think I didn't care if they ever found the killer, and that wasn't true. Murder is the scariest thing there is, especially when the guy who did it was still out there someplace, walking around.

The best way to keep from worrying about something is to keep busy doing stuff you like. I didn't want to think about the murder, so I was lying on the floor of our big front room, the newspaper spread in front of me, looking for stories about my father. He's a lawyer, the kind who works for people who are supposed to have broken the law. Sometimes he takes murder cases, so there are always a couple of articles a month where he's quoted. "Defence counsel Gordon March questions police procedures." Stuff like that.

When I heard Mom and Raffi thundering up the stairs, I jumped up to open the door. Mom staggered into the apartment with a zillion bags of groceries. Raffi followed with two cases of pop, a case of little apple juice cartons, a three-litre bag of milk, and a huge box of laundry detergent.

"Tammi's back," Mom said. "Poor Tammi. She must be sad."

Raffi grabbed six cans of Diet Coke, lined them up on the counter like little soldiers, and then transferred them to the fridge. Then he took another from the carton, snapped it open and drained half of it in one gulp. He jiggled the remainder around in the can. "She didn't seem all that sad to me," he said. "More nervous, I'd say."

I started putting the cold stuff away. "Nervous about what?" I asked.

"Good question," Raffi said. "Why is Tammi nervous? You agree she's nervous, Lynda?"

Mom nodded. "She's nervous."

"Maybe she's a suspect," Raffi said.

I stared at him, hard. "Tammi? A suspect? That's nuts! There was a guy there, arguing with Ray. There was a big fight!"

Raffi tossed his empty can into the garbage. I sighed noisily, picked it up, shook it off, and dropped it into the recycling box. "I wish I had a quarter for every time I've done that," I muttered.

"Not every argument leads to murder," Raffi said. "If it did, the two of you'd have killed me fifty times over."

Sometimes Mom acts like Raffi isn't even in the room with us. She did that now. "Tammi wants to talk to you, Jess," she said. "I think it's about babysitting. She said something about going to bingo tonight."

"Tonight!" I said. My face tightened up like some giant pinched it.

"You have a problem with that, Jess?" Raffi asked. When Mom ignored him, he ignored that he was being ignored. Adults can be really weird.

I opened my mouth to say something, then closed it again, because I didn't know how I felt. I needed the money I got from babysitting, but did I really want to go to a place where someone I know was killed?

"I said I'd ask you to go down," Mom said. "To talk to her."

"Mom!"

"Mmm?" She was standing on a chair, rearranging the cupboard over the sink.

"What will I say? I mean, Ray's dead! I can't just walk in there as if nothing happened!"

She climbed back down, and sat on the chair, looking thoughtful. "Well, you should say something, I suppose. *I'm sorry* would be fine. I wouldn't worry about it."

"What did you say?" I asked.

She looked at Raffi and frowned. "I know I gave her a hug, but ..."

"You said, *Poor Tammi, how awful for you*," Raffi said. "And I, sensitive, new-age guy that I am, said, *Yeah, Tammi, bad stuff.*"

"I just know I'll come out with something really dumb," I said. "Something really ignorant. How am I supposed to know what to say, or what not to say? Nobody ever tells kids this stuff."

"Ah," Raffi said. "I hear you."

Mom poked a straw into a box of apple juice. She looked from Raffi to me, and from me to Raffi. "Oh-oh," she said. "I can see where this is leading."

Raffi took a little walk around the room, bouncing on his toes like he did when he was thinking. "I'd like to help you out, Jess," he said. "But I don't know. The minute I tell you what not to say, tell you what's really ignorant, you and Lynda'll dump all over me." He folded his arms over his head, and looked scared, as if we were going to beat on him, with sticks.

"Do we do that?" I asked Mom. "Dump on him?"

"Not us," she said. "We're completely supportive. He says something stupid, we never even tell him."

"Yeah, I said. "We just tell each other." I was trying not to grin, but my face wouldn't cooperate.

"You two!" Raffi said. "What's a guy to do? OK, here we go."

One of the things Raffi does, one of his talents, is acting. When he moved to stand in the doorway, it was hard to believe I wasn't watching a short girl, instead of a tall man.

"You're down in her apartment, Jess," he said. "Sort of circulating around the room. You know, looking at things, checking them out?" Shoulders hunched, his head lowered between them, he prowled around the living room. "Tammi?" he said, his voice high like a woman's, "Tammi?"

Then he switched to his own deep tone. "You sure you won't be mad at me now?"

Mom was smiling, but I was serious. I really wanted to know what he'd say. "I won't be mad, I promise. Cross my heart."

He nodded. "Tammi?" he said, in his gravelly high squeak. "Not to worry, Tammi. You'll find another guy real soon. Easy come, easy go."

"Yetch!" Mom yelled. "Raffi, that's gross! That's disgusting!"

Raffi held his hand up, as if he was stopping traffic. "Not done yet," he said. He bent to look under the table, then tipped a chair up to examine the seat. "Tammi?" he said. "Is this it? Is this where Ray croaked? Is this..." He lowered his voice a little, pretending to be horrified. "Is this ... dried blood?"

Mom made gagging sounds in her throat, as if she was trying not to throw up. "You are too much Raffi," she said. "Too much. Twisted, that's what you are."

Raffi nodded. "And insensitive," he said. "And offensive. That's what I was. Believe me Jess, you've got nothing to worry about. You couldn't say anything that bad if I wrote you a script."

I grinned. "You're right," I said. "I couldn't. I feel pretty weird about babysitting down there, though. Do you think I should go?"

"It's up to you," Mom said. "I don't feel strongly one way or the other. You may feel a bit spooked, but there can't be any danger. I mean, Tammi was right there and the murderer didn't touch her. Just let her know, Jess."

"She'll talk me into it, I know she will. I mean, what can I say? I *don't want to come, Tammi. I'm too chicken?*"

Mom thought for a minute. "Why don't you ask Flavia to go with you?" she said.

I practised what I was going to say to Tammi all the way down the stairs. Then I knocked. Maybe she wouldn't be there. Maybe I'd be lucky.

"Hi," she said.

She could have been Tammi's big sister, or her aunt, or even her mother, but I knew she wasn't. She was Tammi, ghostly pale, tired, and a whole lot older. Her clothes were different too; black tailored slacks, and a baggy turtle-neck, also black. No more dangling earrings, no short skirt, no fancy tights and, the biggest surprise of all, no scoop-necked, body-hugging sweater. Even her hair had changed. It was still orange with dark roots, but it didn't stick out all over her head any more. It was pulled back, in some kind of a twist, sort of like Mom's.

"You look so different!" I gasped. Then I remembered my manners. "Uh, Tammi, I'm ..."

"Do I look all right?" she said, spreading her arms to give me a better view. "I'm a widow, after all. Gotta dress the part." Without waiting for an answer, she pointed to a spot on the floor where there used to be a rug. "There," she said. "He was killed right there. In case you're wondering, and like, don't wanna ask. Anyhow I thought I'd go to bingo tonight, just to get out, you know? Tongues will wag, probably, it being so soon and all. Like I'm looking for another guy? But I'm not, so I don't care. If I don't get away from that kid for a couple of hours I'll go positively squirrelly. It's like she knows, or something. Just never stops fussing."

A surprisingly loud yowl echoed down the hall. "Speaking of which," Tammi said. "Comin', love," she yelled. "Just hold onto your diaper! Thanks, Jess. Quarter to seven, OK? S'cuse me."

The door closed quietly but firmly in my face. Mom was right. I didn't need to worry about what to say.

CHAPTER 6

"This is one crabby baby," I said.

Brianna, a tiny redhead with pale skin and big blue eyes, was propped on the couch beside me. Flavia, who was crouched on the floor in front of us, played peek-under-a-blanket. I wiggled a Minnie Mouse doll so it danced on my lap, but nothing worked. When Brianna's lower lip began to wobble, I picked her up.

"She's tired," I said. "Let's put her to bed."

We checked her diaper on the changing table, then I carried her over to the crib. For somebody so young, Brianna's pretty smart. The minute she saw that bed, she started to shriek. I hesitated and looked at Flavia, who made a stern face and pointed to the mattress. Brianna clutched at my hair and shrieked even louder. I pried her little hands away and put her down.

"Maybe she'll stop when we leave the room," Flavia said.

Back in the living room, I sat stiffly on the edge of the couch while Brianna screamed hysterically. After about two minutes I went back into the bedroom and picked her up. She sighed, whimpered a little, then hiccuped; her face was pink and triumphant. Tears glistened in her eyelashes as I carried her into the kitchen, where I warmed a bottle of milk.

The TV program we were watching was a rerun of some violent cop show which was totally nauseating, but it gave us something to talk about. Not that Flavia is hard to talk to, she isn't. I was the problem. All I could think about was Sheena's question. If I didn't ask it, I'd feel like I'd let Sheena down. If I did ask it, I'd feel bad about that, like I was spying on the Lopezes. So I cheated. I told the truth.

"You remember Sheena, that cop that was here?" I said.

"The one we met?" Flavia asked.

"Yeah. Well, she wanted me to ask you something about the night of the murder."

Flavia took the nipple out of Brianna's mouth and adjusted the top of the bottle. "The milk's coming out too fast," she said. "She'll get gas."

"You could burp her," I said. "Well, anyway, Sheena can't figure out how come no one in your family heard anything. Especially after I told her how big a fight there was."

Flavia kept on fiddling with the suction in the bottle. Brianna was sound asleep.

"So she kind of suspects that somebody isn't telling the truth," I said. "Either me, or your whole family."

For several long seconds Flavia didn't answer. Then she sighed. "It's my parents," she said. "They had bad experiences with the police in our country. They were not ... worthy of our trust. So my father is not happy to have us talk to the police here, even though everyone tells us they are not the same at all."

"But you heard something?"

"Yes," she answered. Her voice was almost cross.

"You heard what I heard?"

"Jess. Do not do this to me. Please. My father has forbidden us to speak."

It was my turn to sigh. "I'm sorry," I said. "It's just ..."

"Oh no!" Flavia said.

"What happened to the lights?" My voice sounded funny, even to me. Total darkness, sudden total darkness, can come as a nasty surprise. The kind of surprise you get when you see a beady-eyed rat behind the garbage can, or a snake slithering across your path.

I don't like the dark. I never have. When I turned thirteen, I was too ashamed to have a babysitter when Mom worked at night, so she got me a flashlight and an extension phone for my room. And I always, always, leave the hall light on. It wasn't really the dark I was afraid of, it was the shadows, and what my imagination made of them. Stuffed animals, cuddly and harmless in the light, became raging beasts, addicted to human flesh. A sweater and a belt hanging in my closet turned into an evil strangler waiting to make his move.

Now I was the babysitter myself. No flashlight, no hall light, and even if I could see the numbers on the phone, I wouldn't know who to call. Cautiously, I felt my way across the room to the window and looked out. "That's weird," I said. "The power is still on across the street, and on both sides of us." I skirted the TV and the table and made my way to the door to the stairs. I opened it, then quickly shut it again. There wasn't a glimmer of light anywhere.

Flavia hadn't spoken since the power went off, but a big burp echoed across the room, followed by a soft laugh. "That was Brianna, not me," she whispered.

"Shh, listen," I said, "I hear something. Someone's knocking at the back door. Maybe it's Tammi."

The three apartments, one on top of each other, are almost identical. Shot-gun apartments, Mom calls them, because if you fired a bullet from one end to the other, it would pass through all the rooms. There are doors, with windows in them, leading from the back bedrooms out onto porches. Wooden stairs connect the porches together, running from the top floor where Mom and I live, to Tammi's in the middle, past the Orellanas' on the ground floor, down to the back yard.

"Why would Tammi come up the back way?" Flavia asked.

"If she forgot her key..."

"She could buzz us."

"Not when there's no power," I said. "But it's too early, she wouldn't be back yet."

"I know," Flavia said. "It is Carlos. Our mother has sent him to rescue us. I will go." She handed Brianna over. "Here, her head is here. She is asleep."

I snuggled the baby's soft sweetness and wondered why Carlos would come up the back way, but I couldn't think of a reason. Flavia's footsteps moved quickly down the hall, as if she knew exactly where she was going.

The crashing sound, bones against wood, was the same noise I heard the night Ray was killed, exactly the same. I didn't know what to do. I wanted to call out to Flavia, to ask if she was OK. But if I did that, I'd wake Brianna, who was crabby enough in the light. So I clutched her into my shoulder and shuffle-walked across the living room towards the entrance to the hall. I stood there, listening. It took me a minute to figure out what had happened. The three apartments have one major difference. The top two, ours and Tammi's, have steps leading down into the back bedroom. Flavia wouldn't know this, because the ground floor, theirs, is all on one level.

I moved slowly down the hall, counting doorways and listening for sounds. When I reached Brianna's room, I felt my way along the wall to the crib, gently lowered her into it, and pulled up the railing. Out in the hall again, I called Flavia. "Where are you? Are you hurt?" I said. I stepped carefully down the three steps into the bedroom. When she put her hand on my arm, I jumped. "Ah!" I said.

"Shush," she whispered.

"I thought you were dead!" I said.

"I almost broke my bottom. There are stairs! But look. Someone is there, at the window in the door. Who is it?"

A head was silhouetted against the light of the city. As we watched, a hand tapped on the glass, one finger at a time.

"It's not Tammi," I said. "It's too big for her. Who do we know who wears a ball cap?"

"It is not Carlos either. He is shorter than I am. What should we do?"

My heart pounded noisily, and my mouth was so dry I could hardly speak. "Maybe it's the murderer, come back to get Tammi," I said.

The head disappeared, then something hard whacked against the glass, which cracked, but stayed in the window. We watched, hypnotized, as the hand, now wrapped in something bulky, pushed its way through. Pieces of glass clattered and tinkled to the bedroom floor. The hand, followed by an arm, inched slowly through the opening towards the bolt on the door.

My body had turned to stone; Flavia had to pull and push me up the steps. "Move!" she hissed. "We have to leave! Fast!"

We stumbled down the hall to the front door, where I stopped dead. "The baby!" I said. "I can't leave! My mother would kill me!"

Flavia shoved me aside. "Then hide," she said. "I will bring Carlos."

A four-month-old baby, asleep, isn't much company when you're terrified. When the screen door in the back bedroom slammed shut and I knew the man was in the apartment, I almost followed Flavia down the front stairs, but I couldn't do it, even though I wanted to more than I've ever wanted to do anything. Instead, I moved quietly back down the hall, counting doors again. Coat closet. Linen closet. Bathroom, the room I needed the most. Baby's room.

I heard him now. Footsteps. There was a light too, a flashlight. So much for hiding. The beam flickered around the back bedroom, then down the hall. Shadows, like birds, fluttered towards me. I tiptoed into the baby's room, and pushed my hands through the slats of the crib, in and out, moving further and further up the mattress. At last, I felt a foot, a tiny foot. She was lying crosswise, at the very top of the bed. I ran my hand up her leg to her warm, gently breathing body and pulled her across the sheet towards me. As I bent over the top of the railing, it dug painfully into my middle. Brianna murmured when I picked her up.

The footsteps came closer and closer, then stopped. He was in the doorway, just a few feet away from me. The beam of the flashlight played around the room, passing me, then moving back, searching me out. I cringed into a corner, there was no other place to go. The light found my face, and blinded me. It glared steadily for what seemed like hours but could only have been seconds. My teeth rattled.

"Don't kill me," I cried. "I'm only the babysitter!"

My knees collapsed under me and I sank to the floor, unsteady with the baby's extra weight. The light followed. This was the end, for both of us. I knew it. He was the murderer, back to bump off the witness to his crime. The innocent person he thought was the witness. The innocent person who was in the wrong place at the wrong time.

Brianna twisted her head away from the light, and whimpered. I held her tighter. My heart pounded wildly in my chest, almost deafening me. Then the man whispered something, or he laughed, I couldn't tell which; a familiar noise, like a gush of air escaping from a half-blown balloon or the hiss of a cornered cat. It was followed by darkness. Steps, running steps, retreated down the hall. The screen door banged shut and heavy thudding noises moved down the stairs, becoming fainter and fainter, until there was silence. Brianna was awake now, and scared. She howled. I covered her with tears of relief.

Then Flavia was back, and behind her, Carlos. They were holding candles stuck in kitchen glasses. Carlos was fierce, with a huge carving knife in one hand and a smaller one in his teeth.

"He's gone," I said. The candlelight was gentle, and hid my face. "We're fine."

CHAPTER 7

After the killer left we paraded carefully down the front stairs to the Orellanas' apartment. As soon as we got there I handed Brianna over to Flavia, and collapsed into the depths of a huge armchair. Mrs. Orellana was lighting more candles, setting them on little saucers and placing them around the room.

Carlos folded his arms over his chest and leaned back against the wall. "Somebody should do something about the lights," he said. "We can't stay in the dark all night."

Was it my imagination or was everybody looking at me? I didn't want to think about the lights. I didn't want to think about anything, but I forced myself to respond. "You can turn the power for the whole building off and on with a big switch," I said. "It's in the basement."

"Where?" Carlos asked.

"If you go down the stairs and keep going," I said, "you'll come to the back wall. The fuse box is right there. It's not hard to find," I added.

Nobody said anything. Nobody volunteered.

What I should have said was *I'm not going*. What I actually said was "I'm not going alone." Sometimes I'm my own worst enemy.
A few minutes later Carlos and I were standing side by side in the front lobby. When I yanked the basement door open, a quick scraping sound echoed up the stairs.

"Something's down there," I whispered.

We stood quietly, listening. "Perhaps it was a mouse," Carlos said. "Or a rat."

We held our candles out in front of us, and even though the stairs were wide enough for two, Carlos let me go ahead. I made my way down, right foot ahead each time, left catching up. On the nineteenth step I felt a change. The railing ended and I stepped onto the cement floor of the basement.

"We're here," I said. "The hall runs from front to back, like in the apartments. There's a fire exit at the other end, but hardly anybody uses it."

On the way to the fuse box we passed the closed doors of the furnace room, the storage room, the garbage room and the laundry room. The laundry room? I moved my candle so I could take a better look. The door was shut. But how could it be, when it was always, always kept open? Wedged open, with a little triangle of wood, because of all the heat and steam.

Panic hit me, hard. The noise I heard when we stood at the top of the stairs wasn't a mouse. It wasn't even a rat. It was the dull scraping sound wood makes when it's dragged over cement; the sound of a door being forced shut, a door that had been propped open for years. My mind was jumping all over the place but I knew one thing for sure. That door hadn't moved by itself.

The man in Tammi's apartment had run down the back stairs, and the back stairs ended right beside the fire exit from the basement. You didn't have to be a genius to figure out who was behind that door.

I made a quick decision. If the murderer wanted to hide in the laundry, that was just fine with me. What I was going to do was turn the power back on. Then I was going to get out of there, as fast as my legs would carry me.

The fuse box was in a cubbyhole near the back door. I held my candle up to it, and pointed to the master switch.

"It is too high to reach," Carlos said. "I will lift you, and you can do it."

I grimaced into the dark. "I'm pretty heavy," I said.

"You are perfect," Carlos said. He put his candle on the floor and squatted beside it.

I climbed onto his back and swung my legs over his shoulders. Carlos grunted. Then he grunted some more, and I swayed upwards until the big switch was right in front of me. It was painted red. I pushed with one hand at the side that was sticking up. Then I pushed again. I couldn't move it. It didn't help that my hand was shaking.

"Can you take my candle?" I said. My voice was shaking too.

Carlos reached up, and as I lowered the glass, the flame blew from side to side and shadows jumped across the wall. I pushed the switch again, really hard, with two hands this time. There was a loud snap, and light poured down from the hall fixture at the top of the stairs. The basement was still dark.

I slid from Carlos's shoulders to the floor. When I stepped away from him, his hand pulled at my arm.

"Jess," he whispered. "Don't go." His hand moved up to my shoulder. "I want to kiss you."

"Now?" I said. I swung my eyes towards the laundry and swallowed hard.

"You did not say *no*," he said. "So I believe you mean *yes*." His face moved towards me and his mouth pressed softly against the side of my mine, sort of half on and half off. Probably I wasn't doing it right, but he didn't seem to mind. When I pulled away, it wasn't because I didn't like kissing him, it was because I couldn't concentrate. I kept listening for that door, for the scraping noise it would make when it opened.

"You can't stop now!" Carlos said.

"I have to!" I answered. It wasn't what I wanted to say. What I wanted to say was *There's a murderer in the laundry*! What I wanted to do was run. So that's what I did.

"Tea, with honey," Mrs. Orellana said. "Perhaps toast too."

I nodded gratefully. Although the Orellanas' apartment was warm, I was having temperature problems. I was hot, then cold, then hot again, or hot with the shivers. Even worse, there were constant replays going on in my head: glass breaking and a hand coming through a window; a light shining in my face; a killer laughing at me.

"We should call the police," I said. "I think that man is still in the building." Then I explained about the laundry door.

Mrs. Orellana set the kettle on the stove, and looked at Carlos, who slouched down in his chair and stared at me through thick eyelashes.

"If that guy was down there, he'll be gone by now," he said. "We should wait and let Mrs. Tammi call. It is her apartment."

Flavia held two pieces of bread suspended over the toaster. She glanced first at her mother, then at me, and nodded in agreement.

I'd left a note on Tammi's door, but we heard her come in. When I went into the hall to meet her, I explained everything that had happened; how the man had broken in, and how I thought he was still in the basement. "We haven't called the cops yet," I added. "We were waiting for you. Do you want to do it now? I could talk to them."

Her face glazed over, as if I was really bugging her. "I'll do it, Jess. I mean, it's my apartment, right?"

"You can't go back there, Tammi," I said. "It's you he's after! Do you want to stay with me?"

She was quiet for a moment. Then she rolled her eyes like I was the dumbest kid alive. "I'll be fine," she said. "I have a gun." She patted her purse. "My friend Terri lent it to me."

Carlos crowded into the doorway. "Show me?" he asked.

Tammi glared at him and shook her head. "No," she said.

That night I slept in Mom's room. There's a door there too, with a window in it, just like at Tammi's. The hall light was on, I'd put a hammer on the night-table beside me, and the phone was beside it, programmed to dial 911 at the push of a button. I was prepared for anything, even a murderer.

I drifted in and out of sleep, fighting it, afraid to let go. Nightmares and flashbacks all twisted together like the strands of a French braid. I heard footsteps on the back stairs, someone tapping at a door, which opened, then closed again. I jumped awake, my heart thumping in my chest, but there was no one there, only the tail-end of a dream. I slept. Then something, or someone, was banging or maybe hammering; it was a familiar sound, one I'd heard before.

I woke to sunlight, and the rich smells of coffee and bacon. Someone was knocking on the bedroom door.

"Jess?" Raffi said. "Want breakfast?"

"Sure. Give me a minute."

"Ten."

I snuggled back into Mom's duvet and thought about the one nice thing that happened; Carlos, and my first kiss ever. I rubbed my mouth with my fingers, wondering how it felt to him, to his lips. Then I kissed the back of my hand, and pretended it was him. I wished he'd tongue-kissed me, because I couldn't figure out how people did it, and whether it was disgusting or not, and there was no one I wanted to ask. Then I pulled the duvet over my head, and thought about him some more, and tried to figure out what we'd do to each other next. It was hard to believe that I finally had a boyfriend, but it felt wonderful. I could hardly wait to tell Kelly.

"Jess," Mom said. "I thought you wanted breakfast. Aren't you hot under there?"

"Yes," I said. "Absolutely. Cooking."

My mother had a cow, of course. A-pacing-up-and-down-the-living-room, clutching-her-elbows-with-her-opposite-hands cow. Not about Carlos and me, because you can't get all upset about something you don't even know about. What got her going was me being in Tammi's apartment and the killer coming back. Not that I blamed her — it got me going too.

"That's it," she roared. "No more babysitting!"

She hadn't been that upset since she and my father had their big fight when I was twelve. "No more babysitting?" I said. "What am I supposed to do for spending money?"

"Use your head, Jess. No more babysitting for Tammi. Oh, I feel so guilty! I should never have let you go, never! You could have been k-k-killed!"

Mom was so nice sometimes, but I wished she wouldn't bawl, it made me feel guilty, like everything was my fault. I put my arm around her. "You couldn't have known," I said.

CHAPTER 8

When I passed the Orellanas' door the next morning, I heard Flavia and Carlos inside getting ready for school, but I couldn't wait for them. I had an appointment with the principal. I was jogging along Jameson, paying no attention to anyone, when I almost bumped into the tall skinny back of Jon Bell. As usual, he was alone.

"Hey, Jess!" he called, as I sprinted by him. "What's the rush?"

I checked my watch, and slowed down. "Mrs. Carelli," I said. "Can't keep her waiting."

"Oh oh."

"No, it's not like that. And she's really nice."

"So if you aren't in trouble, what's ... or am I being too nosy?"

"It's sort of embarrassing," I said. "I'm reporting someone for harassing me."

"The Roach?"

My mouth dropped open. "How did you know?"

"I heard him the day you did your book report in English. I followed you into the hall. I wanted to say something, but you took off, so ... I didn't. What he said to you was complete garbage. I mean, you're not heavy at all. You look just right to me."

How do you answer someone who says you're not fat when you *know* you are? "Uh, thanks," I said.

"You're on your way to report him now? This minute?"

I nodded.

"Do you want me to come? It might help. I heard everything he said."

I looked up at him, eyeball to eyeball, even though I had to stretch my neck to do it. "Wow!" I said. "Great!" I checked my watch again. "We're a few minutes early. Do you want to stay outside?"

"Sure."

We found an empty bench by the day-care playground. When Jon sat, his knees folded up just like a grasshopper's. I slipped my knapsack off my shoulder, and leaned back, tilting my head to catch the sun. I was wearing tights, and a short skirt. I have nice legs. I crossed them.

"How come you know Mrs. Carelli?" he said. "Have you reported the Roach before?"

"No. I was in her office on the day of the murder, when a cop came to ask me to make a statement." I looked at his face as we talked. One of the nice things about Jon is that he never tries to be cool. I uncrossed my legs and tucked them under the bench.

"What murder?" he said. "The one a couple of weeks ago over on Telrose?"

I nodded. "It was in the apartment underneath us. The whole thing's pretty weird."

"Hey!" he said. "Could we talk about it sometime? I'm really interested in stuff like that." Then he frowned. "Unless it makes you feel bad? I don't want to make it seem like a joke."

I looked at him some more. "No, that would be good," I said. I almost mentioned Flavia and Carlos, and Kelly, but I didn't. Flavia and Carlos were too weird about the cops, and Kelly hardly even had time for me any more.

"Hey, it's time to go," I said. "I don't want to keep Mrs. Carelli waiting. Are you sure you want to do this?"

"Absolutely," he said. "Absolutely."

I'd hadn't told my mother about the Roach, so that evening when we were chopping vegetables for a stir-fry, I decided I'd better come clean.

"Why didn't you tell me before?" she said. "This is the same guy, isn't it? The one who did all those awful things in public school?"

I nodded. Ronny Roach has been making me upchuck my lunch since grade three. That was the year of the little pink plush jewel-box coffins. The dead mice inside had not died natural deaths, and they hadn't been killed in mouse-traps either. There was too much dried blood for that. One had its throat sliced straight across. The other was missing all four tiny feet.

Ronny didn't improve with age. In grade five someone caught him torturing a cat. In grade six he set fire to a Sri Lankan girl's braid with a cigarette lighter. After that he was away for a while, locked up somewhere. When he came back for grade eight we were in the same class. That's when I became his sworn enemy for life.

It happened when I was waiting for my father to pick me up for what turned out to be one of our last every-second-weekend visits. I was sitting on the school steps, feeling really awful about my parents' latest fight, when Natalie, a girl with waist-length black hair, came out the main door. Ronny Roach was just behind her.

When they reached the sidewalk, a whole lot of things happened at the same time. Dad's car pulled up at the curb. Ronny's hands, holding a long thin pair of scissors that glittered in the late afternoon sun, darted towards the back of Natalie's neck and started to hack off her hair somewhere around her ears. I jumped up and screamed blue murder.

Natalie comes from India and because of her religion her hair had never been cut in her whole life, so it wasn't just a beauty-destroying thing Ronny did, which would have been terrible enough, but something much, much worse.

Ronny flung the scissors to the ground and took off down the street. My father called the police on his car phone. I picked up the big hunk of hair from the sidewalk and handed it back to Natalie, who was sobbing hysterically and trying to cover the shorn part of her head with her hands.

Neither Natalie nor Dad could identify Ronny by name, but I could, and I did. So when he got sent to the Juvenile Detention Centre for the second time, he blamed me.

"You'd better be careful, Jess," Mom said. "He's trouble."

Raffi looked serious. "Maybe I'll have a little talk with him," he said. "What do you think Lynda? Jess? Should I do that?"

"Go for it," Mom said. "Just don't threaten him. Threatening is a crime."

Raffi bent his arm up, caressed his biceps and raised his eyebrows. "Who me?" he said. "You think I'd threaten somebody? Jess, you didn't answer. Should I, er, have a little chat with this guy?"

"I guess," I said. "It can't hurt. Is it OK if Jon comes over Saturday afternoon for a while?"

Raffi dropped a huge handful of noodles into a pot of boiling water. "Jon who?" he said.

"Jon Bell," I said. "My friend." I emphasized the word *friend*.

Mom raised her eyebrows in a way I loathe, but I guess I asked for it. "F-r-i-e-n-d," I said.

"Oh," she said. "Sure."

I could feel the blush creeping up my neck. When the phone rang she wiped her hands on her jeans, and answered. "For you," she said and handed me the phone. "It's Sheena."

"Hi," I said. "I was going to call you."

"What's up, duckie? You talk to the Orellana kids yet?"

"Well, I tried. But I didn't get an answer. And what with the break-in and all..."

"What break-in?"

"Tammi phoned, to report it," I said. "It was in her apartment. The night before last."

"Hang on a minute, will you?"

When Sheena came back on the line her voice was abrupt and furious. "No report," she said. "You gonna be there for a while? I'll come over."

"Sure. But we're just going to eat."

"Half an hour?"

"Three-quarters would be better," I said. When I hung up, I looked at Raffi.

"She's coming over, I said. "Half to three-quarters of an hour."

"I'm out of here," Raffi said.

"So what happened?" Sheena's notebook was open, her pen poised. "Start from the beginning."

I told her the whole story. The blackout, the break-in, the scene in Brianna's room. I also mentioned the closed laundry door in the basement.

"Did you get a look at this guy, Jess?"

"No. It was dark. The only thing I saw was the side of his head, when he was standing at the back door."

"There was a light on behind him?"

"Just the sky, but it seemed sort of bright."

"Enough to identify him, say, in a line-up?"

"No," I said. "Only enough to know he's big."

"How big?" she asked. "Big as me?"

"Hmm," I said. "He came up nearly to the top of the window in the back door."

"You have a door like that here?"

I nodded.

"Let's have a look then," she said.

We walked single-file down the hall, Mom first, me next, and Sheena last. I stood where I'd stood in Tammi's apartment when I saw the man's silhouette. Then I pointed out how high his head came on the window. Sheena went outside and stood in front of the door. Her head came to almost the same place.

"He's about as tall as you are," I said.

"Six-one," she muttered, and wrote it down. "Any feeling for how heavy he is?"

I shook my head. "I was pretty scared, actually."

"Not surprised. And you said the Orellana kids aren't talking?"

"No," I said. "Not yet."

"Gal's gotta do what a gal's gotta do," she said.

"What's that?" I asked.

"Take them in for questioning. Some of them anyway. Now, about Mrs. Bird. Did she seem scared when you told her about this guy? Apprehensive about going back to her apartment?"

I hunched my shoulders. I hated talking about Tammi, and Sheena knew it. "Tammi wasn't scared because she had a gun," I said. "Her friend Terri lent it to her."

"Did you see it?"

"No," I said.

"And Mrs. Bird indicated that she would call the police?"

I nodded. "Maybe she just forgot?"

Sheena groaned. "I doubt it," she said. "Still, she's a pretty spaced-out woman, so who knows what she'd do. Is she down there now?"

"I think so," I said. "I heard the baby crying just before you came."

Sheena pushed herself out of her chair. "One other thing," she said. "What can you tell me about a guy named," she flipped some pages in the notebook, "Raphael Morgan?"

"Raffi?" Mom said. Her voice sounded like she was struggling for breath. "He's a friend."

"Does he live here?" Sheena gave me a particularly piercing look.

"No." Mom swung her eyes towards me.

Sheena nodded. "We had a report that he's around here a lot," she said.

Mom hugged herself. "He lives across the street," she said.

"Which building?" Sheena went to the window and pointed. "That one?"

"Apartment three," Mom said. Her voice was very small.

CHAPTER 9

It was just like Kelly said, having a boyfriend changes your life. The way I walked, the way I talked, the way I wore my clothes, how fat I felt, everything was different.

After that night in the basement, I couldn't get Carlos out of my head: the soft pressure of his lips; the way his eyes hooded over, making promises. Something would happen soon. I knew it.

As the days went by, I couldn't understand why he was taking so long. Didn't he *want* to kiss me again? Didn't he like me? Did I scare him away? Maybe he was shy, or couldn't get away from his parents, or didn't want them to know about us. That would be difficult, under the circumstances. Or maybe I was supposed to go to him.

It was a Friday night, and I was alone. Mom and Raffi had gone to a party. Tammi and Brianna had disappeared again, and I thought I'd heard the Orellanas go out, the whole family. So the soft tapping on the back door came as a shock. It was Carlos, his hand shading his eyes, peering in the window.

I stepped outside, onto the porch. It was dusk, a soft May evening. We sat on the top step, three stories above ground, and looked down over the neighbourhood. A sprinkler waved back and forth in someone's yard. A young girl chained a bicycle to a porch railing. Pink streaks of cloud coloured the sky and the promise of summer floated through the air.

Darkness crept over the city. Carlos' arm was warm against my shoulders. We kissed, properly this time. His mouth tasted of toothpaste. "Lie down," he whispered. I could still see his eyes, the whites. "Please," he said. My toes wiggled.

I touched the softness of his hair, then lay back, ignoring the hard wood beneath me. Feeling his hands on my face, my neck. We kissed again. A gentle kiss. Perfection.

Then suddenly, too suddenly, his hands were all over me, totally out of control. His lips turned hard, and pushed against my teeth, and his tongue choked me. I shoved him away.

"What's wrong?" he said. He didn't sound happy.

"You're hurting me!"

"I am? How?"

"Your mouth. Everything." I struggled to my feet, but he followed, holding my arm, holding it too tight. Bricks dug into my back as he squashed me into the wall.

He groaned. "You don't want to?" he said.

His hands grabbed roughly at my clothes and his breathing was funny, like he'd just run a race. I felt wild and scared and wonderful and dizzy, all mixed up together. I thought about Kelly, how far she was ahead of me, knowing everything, all the mysteries of sex. Almost all the mysteries. I wondered which of us would stop being a virgin first.

"C'mon, Jess," he said. His voice was low and smooth and pleading. "Let's do it. It'll be so nice. You'll love it."

As he squeezed against me, something hard pressed into my belly button. "I don't think I'm ready for this," I said.

"It won't hurt. And I'll be careful, I promise."

Careful. That word. It stung me.

"No," I said. "I don't want to."

I needed Kelly, needed her badly, and Carlos hadn't been gone two minutes before I was on the phone, looking for her. I had all these questions, and who could I ask but her?

Lately, every time I needed her, she wasn't there, and this was no different. She wasn't there that Friday night, she wasn't there Saturday, and she wasn't there Sunday. No one was, so they were all away somewhere. And on Monday, she cut school.

When classes were over I crossed Queen at Jameson, headed west for a block, then north. It's a quieter neighbourhood than where we live, and there are fewer people. Probably because there are hardly any apartment buildings.

Three blocks north of Queen I turned into a small house with a large porch. It was a pretty nice place, if you could ignore the Pain. The Pain's real name is Melissa, and she's ten.

Kelly wasn't at home. The Pain was, and so was Mrs. Curran.

"I don't know, Jess," she said. "Kelly's spending an awful lot of time with that Joey person. Did you miss her at school?"

"Uh, we hardly ever have the same classes, Mrs. Curran," I said. This was true, sort of.

"She skipped, didn't she?" the Pain said.

Mrs. Curran shook her head from side to side. "That girl will be the death of me, I'm sure," she said. "And if she isn't, missy, you will be. Now scoot. Upstairs with you. I want to talk to Jess."

"She won't tell you anything," the Pain said. "She and Kelly have secrets."

"You'll stay, won't you, Jess? I'll just put the kettle on and we'll have a nice chat."

Mrs. Curran's idea of a nice chat was quizzing me about Kelly. "Uh, I have to make supper," I said. This was true. I mean, I don't *have* to make it, but it's what I do. "I just wanted to borrow a book," I said. "But I'll catch her tomorrow."

The Pain hung over the stairs, then stretched one leg down along the banister, as if it was a parallel bar. "You'll catch her tomorrow *if* she goes to school," she said.

On my way home I crossed Queen again, then cut through the schoolyard beside the gym. I was thinking so hard about Kelly, and about why she didn't want to be friends with me any more, that I almost crashed right into Carlos. Carlos and a girl. They were standing on the sidewalk just a few feet in front of me, too busy kissing to notice anyone but each other. The girl had long, very dark hair, tight jeans, and a perfect body. I hated her.

I hated him even more. I wished I'd never laid eyes on him. I wished I never had to see him again in my whole life.

I backed up, around the corner of the building. What I really wanted to do was scream, right there in the school yard, just scream and scream and scream. My eyes were squeezed shut and my fingernails were digging into the soft part of my palms. I was leaning back against the outside wall of the gym. Carlos couldn't see me, but other people could. I took a deep gasping breath, and then I took another. I felt awful, worse than I'd ever felt in my whole life, like I'd just had a barbecue skewer stuck through my heart, but I knew I'd feel even worse if I saw anybody I knew. It was time to get out of there. I slipped around the corner of the school and ran home the other way.

I would have told Kelly everything, every intimate detail, if she'd been around. Maybe having no friends was a good thing. At least I didn't have to be embarrassed in front of anybody except myself. And him.

CHAPTER 10

Jon worked Saturday mornings, so he was coming over Saturday afternoon to talk about the murder.

The apartment was a mess. Cleaning it is Mom's job, not mine, but I picked up the newspapers, took out the garbage and did the dishes. Jon lived in a really nice-looking house, with only one mailbox. I didn't think he was the kind of person who'd let that sort of thing matter, but a quick tidy-up wouldn't hurt.

I changed into clean jean cut-offs and a black T-shirt. Then I sat at the table and made some notes about the murder. I started writing down everything I could remember that didn't make sense.

Jon was one minute early. When he lowered his backpack to the floor, he looked around the room, then moved over to the couch, towards the portrait of me that Raffi painted.

"Who did it?" he said.

"A friend of my mom's. Her boyfriend, actually. He took some pictures, and did most of it from them. I only had to sit for him a couple of times."

"It's good."

I waved my arm towards the table. "Want to sit down?"

While I took two cans of pop from the fridge, he fished around in his pack. "Here," he said, and handed me some newspaper clippings. "You probably saw these."

They were write-ups about the murder, and I hadn't. I read them quickly. They didn't say anything I didn't know.

"There are so many strange things going on," I said. I shifted the notes I'd made across the table so they lay between us. "I wrote some of them down. Most of them have to do with Tammi," I said.

"She's the wife, was the wife, of Ray, who got killed." I ticked off the important points on my fingers: the fight, the heavy body falling to the floor while it was still dark, Tammi crying and talking to someone for such a long time after that.

"Wow!" he said. "So she was there when her husband was murdered? Then she knows who did it!"

"She has to know, but she sure isn't telling. And what she is telling has to be the biggest bunch of lies I've ever heard. First, she said she didn't see the guy, that Ray had so many visitors she never even bothered to see who was there. And Ray never had visitors, never. Second, she said she didn't even know Ray was dead until she woke up in the morning."

"After she was crying all night? After the big fight?"

"Yeah."

"Wow," he said. "You think she did it? Did she like this guy or what?"

I shrugged. "Yes and no," I said. "He beat her up at least once, and was really sarcastic, but ..."

"But ..."

"This is sort of embarrassing."

"If we're serious about what we're doing, we have to say what we think. Besides, I'll probably be more embarrassed than you."

I laughed, but just a little, because I could see that was probably true. "They banged away on their bed a lot, like it would hit the wall when they were ... you know. Which was almost every night. I wasn't *listening*, but I couldn't help hearing."

A faint tinge of colour stained his cheeks. "So she liked him. Do you think she could have killed him?"

"No. Partly because she's so little and he was a really big guy, but also because of the fight with the other man. I'm sure he did it, whoever he is. The other strange thing is that Tammi doesn't seem very upset. I mean, if the person you were married to was killed, wouldn't you be really broken up about it? A week later, this woman was going to bingo!"

Jon looked serious. "They must have really loved each other once. Too bad, eh?"

"Yeah. Like my parents. My mom hates my father." I heard my words, but I couldn't believe I'd said them. I never talked about my father to my friends. Never.

Jon looked sad, but he didn't say anything. That was good, because if he had, I probably would have started crying. I almost did anyway.

"There's a lot more weird stuff about this murder," I said. "I didn't have time to write everything down."

"So tell me." He leaned back in the chair, tilting it dangerously. His legs stretched right to the other side of the table.

"Well, after the murder, Tammi went to visit her friend, for, I don't know, just a few days. When she came back she'd changed her style. Totally changed it. You'd hardly know she was the same person. I mean, she looks like my mother now."

"What was her style before?"

"Oh, hot stuff! Hair sticking out all over the place, like she went to bed when it was wet, and never combed it in the morning. And her clothes! Spike heels, really short skirts, plunging necklines." It was my turn to blush this time. Jon didn't seem to notice.

"She wouldn't want to dress like that now. She's in mourning."

"Maybe. I don't know. She's dressed like a widow, but she doesn't seem particularly sad. She seems like herself, but in different clothes."

"That isn't necessarily a clue, is it?"

"I think not being upset is a clue. My mom thinks she's scared, or at least she was when she first came back. I don't think she is, but I have to tell you another long story to explain that."

"This is so exciting. Don't you feel kind of nervous with all that going on underneath you?"

I laughed my best woman-of-the-world laugh, and ran my hand through my hair. "Just wait until you hear the rest of it," I said.

I started by telling him about the night Flavia and I babysat. But I had to interrupt that to tell him about the Orellana family and how Sheena (I had to explain about her too) thinks they're hiding something. It took the best part of an hour before I'd explained everything well enough.

"So that's it," I said. "So far."

"Wow! You were right. The whole thing is pretty wild. What gets me most is that Tammi wasn't scared to go back to the apartment after that guy broke in. And didn't call the cops."

Sometimes when you tell somebody something, you understand it better yourself. "You know what?" I said. "Tammi and that killer are in this together."

"Ah," Jon said. "A triangle. The boyfriend who killed the husband to get the wife."

I sat still for a minute, thinking. "It all comes together," I said. "If she knows him, and is protecting him, everything makes sense. It explains why she wasn't killed, even though she probably witnessed what happened."

"And the talking and the crying in the night. That's because he was still there!"

"She didn't call the cops until morning, to give him time to get away!"

"Of course," Jon said. "But if he's her boyfriend, why did he need to break in the night you were babysitting?"

"And why did he turn off the power? Assuming it was him." I added.

We sat there, sort of looking at each other, but not really actually looking because our eyes weren't focusing on anything. Then Jon grinned. "I've got it," he said. "So nobody would see him come to visit, of course."

"But we haven't figured out why he broke in."

"How about this? He expected her to be there, and she wasn't, so rather than hang around where he could be seen, he went in. And found you."

"Yes," I said. "And she didn't call the cops!"

"And isn't scared to stay there."

"You know what?" I said. "I just realized something else. Something happened the night after the break-in, well, it was the same night really. Mom was at work, so I was alone. My nerves were totally fractured because of everything that happened, and I wasn't sleeping very well. I thought I was sort of dreaming and waking up, but now I wonder if I was really asleep at all. Anyhow, what I think I heard was somebody coming up the back stairs, and then these banging noises, which seemed sort of familiar. But if that guy is Tammi's boyfriend, and he really came back, after hiding out in the basement, the noises I heard could have been ..."

Jon said it for me. "The bed hitting the wall. She must really like bed-bangers."

I shrugged. "I don't know anything about stuff like that."

"Neither do I," he said. "I'd have to know somebody really, really well to ..., you know, do that."

"That's how I feel too," I said.

CHAPTER 11

It was warm outside, but the school was cold, and dank. I was wearing a white long-sleeved cotton shirt with the big cuffs rolled back. There were goose-bumps on my arms.

"So are you going out with this Jon guy, or what?" Kelly said.

"We're just friends. It was nice of him to help me report the Roach."

"Oh oh," Kelly said. "Speak of the devil. Do you see who I see?"

We were walking down the hall, on our way to math class. Ronny Roach was coming towards us. He'd be hard to miss: grimy jeans, bagged out at the knees; a colourless T-shirt, heavily splotched with something green; and an old army shirt, so stiff with dirt it could stand up alone.

"Did the principal talk to him yet?" Kelly said.

"Yeah. He's supposed to apologize."

"Has he?"

"Nope."

"You think he'll do it now?"

"It has to be in writing."

"Well, at least he's stopped hassling you," she said. "Hasn't he?"

"I haven't seen him around since Raffi talked to him. I guess he's been skipping."

I kept hoping he'd turn in to a classroom before we had to meet, but we were too close together by now, that wasn't going to happen. "I'm not ready for this," I said. Even ten feet away, I could see he was mad enough to spit.

We didn't speak as we passed, but his face was pure poison, his eyes so hot with fury they almost smoked. No one had ever looked at me like that before, with such hatred. It surrounded me, like some hideous cloud I couldn't get away from and couldn't ignore.

"If looks could kill," I said, "I'd be dead meat."

CHAPTER 12

Flavia and I were sitting on the wide wooden steps in front of our building. It was five o'clock but the sun was still strong. Carlos and Mr. Orellana, both wearing dress shirts and black trousers, had just left. They were obviously in a hurry, but I didn't think that was the reason Carlos wouldn't look at me, or why his eyes slid past my face.

"Mrs. Tammi thinks you are trying to make trouble for her," Flavia said. "With the police."

I shook my head. "I'm not trying to get her in trouble!" Then I explained what happened. "Sheena phoned," I said. "To find out if you told me anything new about the night of the murder. I told her you didn't, and I mentioned the break-in, sort of like an excuse. I didn't know Tammi hadn't reported it," I added.

"Carlos thinks you are trying to get us in trouble too," she said.

"How can he think that? What have I done?"

"That is not what I believe, Jess," she said. "Carlos is strange sometimes. Did he... did he do anything to you when you were in the basement that night?"

I hid my face in my hands. "How did you know?"

"I saw how he looked at you when you came back upstairs." She paused, as if she was thinking what to say next. "Carlos is very nice about many things. But I must tell you something. He is not at all nice with girls. I have always told my friends to stay away from him."

"He isn't even talking to me now."

"He is angry, because he and our father are on their way to the police station, for an interrogation."

I sighed. "If you'd just said what you heard that night, this wouldn't be happening."

"I told you, our father forbade us to speak of it. You do not have a father?"

"I have one, but I never see him."

"You do not wish to?"

"When I used to see him, Mom got really upset."

"They made a mess," she said, "but it hurt you."

"I'm not hurt." My eyes were watering. Pollen, probably.

"Then why are you crying?" she asked.

Sometimes I forget that Flavia is almost eighteen. "I'm crying because Tammi thinks I'm against her," I said. "And because Carlos hates me because I wouldn't ..."

A police car rolled quietly down the street and pulled up on the sidewalk across from us.

"Jess," Flavia said, "you can not let someone as... silly as Carlos hurt you."

I hardly heard her, I was so busy watching the cops. There were two of them. The big one put his hand on his gun as he closed the cruiser door. He stood there for a while, waving his hands around, explaining something to his buddy. Then the buddy walked quickly down the path between the two apartment buildings and disappeared behind one of them. When he came out on the other side of it, he waved. The big guy, the one by the car, waved back, then headed inside the same building, through the front entrance.

"That's where Raffi lives," I said. I pulled a hangnail off my finger with my teeth. "But they could be after anyone." My eyes were glued to that doorway and my legs and arms felt twitchy. "I need to get up and move around," I said. "Do you think I should go over there?"

"No." Flavia reached her hand out towards me.

The second cop, the smaller one, came at a run from around the back, unlocked the cruiser, and leaned inside. The radio buzzed with static and voices, then was silent. He slammed the car door shut, then disappeared behind the building again.

Neighbours were filtering outside to watch. About ten minutes later, a second cop car, lights flashing, turned the corner, and pulled up behind the first. Two more cops, one of them Sheena, hurried up the walk and went inside. A moment later she was out again, running towards the back yard.

We waited for what seemed like a long time. Then the big cop backed out the front door, gun in hand. Two others, bracketing a large black guy, followed. The large black guy was Raffi. He was wearing handcuffs.

I stood, then moved down the steps, down the sidewalk towards him, as if I was in a dream. Flavia had taken my arm, the way you'd take an old person by the arm, to help him cross the street. She was trying to hold me back, but nothing could do that. I stopped in the middle of the road, and called out to him.

"Raffi? What should I do?"

He looked up and when our eyes locked, he shrugged. Then Sheena opened the car door and motioned him into the back seat. As he bent over to get in, she put her hand on the top of his head. A second cop followed him inside. Doors slammed shut, and they were gone.

Flavia followed me indoors, and stood watching as I ran up the stairs. "If you need anything..." she said.

I headed straight for the phone, to tell Mom. It rang a long time, and someone else answered. Mom wasn't available.

"Not available?" I said. "I'm her daughter! It's an emergency!"

"Oh dear, I'm sorry. She's at a conference today. At some hotel downtown."

I groaned. Mom told me about that, but I wasn't paying attention. "Do you know where?" I asked.

"I don't, but let me ask around," the woman said. "I'll put you on hold."

She was gone a long time. When she came back I knew right away she couldn't help me. "I'm so sorry, dear, no one seems to know exactly where it is. The people who would know are all at the conference. Is there anything I can do?"

"You don't know when it's over?"

"I'm sorry."

"Thanks," I said.

I hung up. Then I sank back into the soft cushions of the couch and closed my eyes. How did life get to be so horrible so fast? Tammi thought I'd ratted on her to the cops. Carlos turned into a creep. Ronny Roach hated me. Kelly had dumped me, and now this!

I phoned Jon. He wasn't there. Then I turned on the TV, but the only choices were kids' shows or news, and I wasn't in the mood for either. I opened the fridge, and looked inside for a while. Then I closed it again. There was a paper attached to the door by a magnet. It was a notice of some meeting for psychiatric nurses at a hotel downtown.

The jerk who answered the phone at the hotel didn't know anything about any nurses' meeting, but after I pleaded with him, he said he'd ask around. Then he cut me off. I called back. He apologized, but it was a fake apology, the kind you make to be polite, not the kind you make when you're sorry. His voice made me want to puke. After about ten minutes of being shifted around from one part of the hotel to another, somebody finally found Mom.

"What's the matter?" she said. She was puffing.

When I told her about Raffi, she started crying. My mother, who never cries, weeping into a phone in some posh downtown hotel.

CHAPTER 13

By the time Mom got home, Raffi had already called from the police station to say he'd been released, and was on his way. He arrived about an hour after she did.

"What I don't understand," Mom said, "is why the Orellanas got invited to go to the police station, and you got dragged off in a cop car."

We were sitting on the back porch, trying out our new wood-and-canvas folding chairs. Mom and Raffi were drinking light beer, the kind you get in the grocery store that has hardly any alcohol. Neither of them are big drinkers. I had my usual, a Diet Coke.

"It's kind of a long story," Raffi said, and grinned what Mom calls his little-kid-with-his-hand-stuck-in-the-cookie-jar grin.

"You did something dumb, didn't you?" Mom said. She was trying to sound mad, but she was so happy to have him back, she couldn't quite bring it off.

I was fooling around with the barbecue. It was just an old charcoal one, but it worked fine. Six small potatoes, the kind with red skins, were wrapped in heavy duty foil, baking away in the coals. While we were waiting for Raffi to get home, I'd marinated some chicken pieces in my special lemon and curry sauce, and they were sizzling away nicely on the grill, smelling wonderful. Mom had made Raffi's favourite salad, with fresh mushrooms and new spinach, to celebrate.

"Yeah, I did something dumb," Raffi said. "Two things." He tilted his head back and took a long swallow of beer. Then he cleared his throat. After that, he looked quickly at Mom, then looked away again.

She exploded. "For goodness' sake, will you just tell us!"

Raffi took another long drink before he answered. "They phoned yesterday," he said. "Just before I went to work. It was that woman, Sheena Bowes. She wanted to see me this morning, at ten. But when I got home last night, after cooking pizza for eight hours, I guess I forgot to set the alarm." He flicked his eyes towards Mom again. "My own fault," he added.

"Uh huh," Mom said. "So you got home about three, right?"

"Right. And I didn't go to sleep for a while. Anyway, when I woke up, the first thing I heard was somebody banging at the door, saying he's a cop. Well, you know how I feel about cops..."

"Oh, Raffi!" Mom said. "You didn't answer?"

"The way I figured it was, they'd think I wasn't there, and after I got up and showered and shaved, I'd call them, and apologize. What I didn't count on was this cop climbing up on the balcony and looking in the window. Ground floor apartments have disadvantages I never even dreamed of."

"Oh Raffi," Mom said again. Then she scrunched her face up like she had a pain in her head.

"So they thought I was being uncooperative..."

"I wonder why," Mom said. "You're lucky they didn't shoot first and ask questions later."

"Well, by now I'm shaking in my boots, or I would have been if I'd had my boots on. And the more scared I got, the less I wanted to open that door. And the longer I didn't, the madder they got. And the less I wanted to ..." As he was telling this, Raffi was acting it out: shaking with pretend fear; swinging his head behind him, then to the front, then behind him again, his eyes huge in his face. "You can see the predicament I was in," he said.

"Why did they call for the second cop car?" I asked.

"Well, I said I'd come out, but only if that Sheena woman was there. So they sent for her. First thing I knew, she was hoisting herself up on the balcony, and peering through the glass door."

"The whole thing could have been prevented if you'd only set your alarm," Mom said.

"Yeah well, I guess you're right," Raffi said. "Anyhow, Sheena saw that I wasn't armed or anything. And when I let her in, she opened the door into the hall."

"They didn't blast in with their guns drawn or anything like that?" Mom said.

"They had their guns drawn, but Sheena was talking to them all the time as she was opening the door, saying she was right in front of it. So everything was cool. Pretty cool. I wasn't in the best shape I've ever been in, but it turned out OK."

"Were they mad at you?" I asked. I stuck a fork into a potato, right through the foil. "They're ready," I said.

"Yeah, they were mad. But they didn't take it out on me. They knew why I was scared. Sheena did, and she talked to them."

The chicken was brown and crusty on one side, so I turned it over. It was boneless, and kind of wiggly. Only one piece fell through the grill, into the coals. The little ones will do that. I fished it out and blew the ashes off.

"Why did they want to talk to you in the first place?" I said. "It's not like you live here."

He sighed. "I'm not sure," he said. "I think it was just routine. Because I'm in and out of here all the time. Because the guy Jess saw down in Tammi's that night was big, like me. I don't know."

"The cops think it was you at Tammi's? The guy who scared me half to death?" I said.

He nodded. "That was mentioned. Maybe they think you're covering up for me because you did it once before, when you told them your mom didn't have a boyfriend."

I groaned, but quietly, inside myself. Raffi was in trouble because I'd acted like a smart-mouthed kid.

"This is ridiculous," Mom said. "You were working the night of the murder, Raffi. You have an alibi. Jess heard that fight at about 2:00 a.m. You couldn't possibly have gotten home until at least three!"

Something changed then, something important. I noticed it right away, even though the only part of Raffi that moved was his eyes. They switched away from Mom, away from me, and looked off somewhere — across back yards, over other apartment buildings, towards the lake. When he spoke his voice was unusually soft. "I only worked till twelve."

"But you work until two, every night!" Mom said.

Raffi sighed, then stood up and circled the porch. When he sat down again he looked at his fingers. They were gripping the arms of his chair. "Not all the time, I don't," he said. "Sometimes I get off early."

Mom's face got sort of hard then, and her voice was pure ice. "You mean you lied?" she said. "You lied to me? And not just once?"

Raffi shut his eyes, and leaned his head back against the brick wall. "That's putting it pretty strongly, Lynda. I mean, I do work till two, most of the time. When I don't, I sometimes visit a friend."

"Freddy," Mom said.

I hadn't met this Freddy, I hadn't even heard of him, but from the sound of Mom's voice, I wasn't sure I wanted to.

"Yeah, Freddy," Raffi said.

"So what is this?" Mom asked. "Am I the warden, or what?"

"Sometimes," he said. "Yeah. Sometimes you are."

I hate it when they fight, so I went inside, got the salad, the plates, and the cutlery, and came back out. Then I helped myself to some of everything. Nobody said a word, but the space around them was heavy with stress. "I think I'll go inside," I said. "Where things are a little more relaxed."

CHAPTER 14

Being around adults who are fighting is the loneliest feeling there is.

I ate the celebration dinner by myself. When I finished, I rinsed off my plate and left it in the sink. Then I headed back down the hall, to see if Mom and Raffi had cheered up any. They hadn't. I could hear them talking through the screen door.

"The trouble with you, Lynda," Raffi said, "is that you always believe the worst about people. There's nothing wrong with Freddy, nothing at all! But you make such a big scene every time I see him ..."

I'm not supposed to eavesdrop, but sometimes I do it anyway, because it's the only way to find out what's going on. I perched on the steps leading down into Mom's bedroom. I couldn't see either of them from there, and unless they got up out of their chairs, they couldn't see me either.

"How can I ever trust you if you're going to sneak around like that?" Mom asked.

"You don't trust me anyhow," Raffi said. "That's what this is all about, isn't it? You think I could have been involved in a murder..." His voice got thick then, like he had a bad cold, but maybe he was crying.

"Of course I don't think you were involved," Mom said. "You'd never do anything like that. I just don't understand why you needed to lie to me. Sure, I made a big deal about you seeing Freddy, but you know why."

"So he smokes a little grass occasionally," Raffi said. "It's not catching, Lynda. I'm not into substances, you know that. You think I'm going to turn into a dope fiend if I hang around with him?"

"You might," Mom said. "If you hang around with people who do dope, you could get in trouble with the cops."

"I've got news for you," Raffi said. "I am in trouble with the cops. I don't have an alibi for the time of the murder."

"I thought you were with Freddy!"

"I went over to his place that night, but he wasn't there. So I came home. All I did then was watch TV for a while, and go to bed."

I'd heard enough. More than enough. I crept down the hall to my room, and lay on my bed, feeling absolutely horrid, like everything was my fault. I only got up once, to clean my teeth and put on my nightgown. Mom and Raffi were still outside, on the porch. They never even said good night.

The next morning, Flavia caught up with me on the way to school. She was extremely cheerful.

"He's back!" she said. "Your mother's friend."

I tried to smile, but I couldn't. "Yeah," I said. "It was a misunderstanding, I guess. He slept in and didn't make his appointment."

"My father and Carlos are very happy this morning also. They told what happened that night, and guess what? No problem!"

"That's good," I said. "What did they hear? The same stuff I did?"

"Yes, like you. The argument, the fight, the crying. But more also. My father had just come back from work, and he saw someone."

"Who?"

"A man. A very large man, like your mother's friend." She looked away from me, then looked back. "Or like Mr. Bird was. That size. It was still dark. My father could not see clearly."

"He can't describe him or anything?"

"The police asked that also. No. A very big man. He can not say more than that."

CHAPTER 15

Jon's house is tall and skinny, just like him. A black iron gate leads into a little courtyard where big clay pots of pink geraniums stand on either side of a bright blue door. It was open and Jon was waiting, watching me come towards him.

The first thing I noticed inside was the smell of apples cooking with cinnamon. The second was the books. Outside a library, I'd never seen so many together in one place. Not just on the shelves, which covered two whole walls of the living room, but all over the place. Piles of them stood on the floor in front of the bookcases, on end tables, leaning into armchairs, even on the couch. There were newspapers too, three or four different ones, and serious-looking magazines.

The walls that didn't have book-cases had paintings. I moved closer to look at them. Thanks to Raffi, I'm not a total ignoramus about art. These were abstracts, really nice ones.

Jon touched one, on the frame. "My mom's. I guess the room's sort of a mess."

"I love it," I said. I wasn't just being polite. It was the best room I'd ever been in.

I followed him through the dining room, where half the table was covered by a computer work station, and two very untidy piles of paper: one hand-written; the other printed. The printed pages had corrections marked on them in red pen. Behind the table there was a china cabinet. It was full of books too.

"They must be in the kitchen," Jon said.

Mr. Bell looked exactly like I expected he would, only older. Long and thin and cheerful-looking, just like Jon, but with greyish, rather than blond hair. Mrs. Bell was a complete surprise. I expected her to be tall and thin too, and elegant and sophisticated. Instead, she was short, shorter even than me, and sort of roly-poly. When she twisted a wisp of dark hair behind one ear and smiled, she looked like one of Santa's elves.

"You'll have some applesauce," she said. "Fresh made." This wasn't a question, it was almost an order, but nobody was taking offence.

We sat on benches at a huge polished wooden table that looked really old. It had gouges all over it, even some black circles from cup rings. While I talked to Mrs. Bell about the cookbooks on the open-shelved cabinet behind us, Jon and his father got into an argument about politics. It was an OK argument; they were listening to each other, but they disagreed. Nothing mean was going on.

After we finished our applesauce, Jon and I went back to the living room to talk about the murder. The only new thing I had to tell him was about Raffi.

"The cops took him away, but ..." I explained how they only did that because Raffi hadn't gone to his appointment. "Then they let him go."

Jon frowned. "He can't be a serious suspect if they let him go," he said.

"He seemed pretty worried to me, I guess because he doesn't have an alibi."

"That doesn't mean he did it," Jon said. "I don't have an alibi either."

"You aren't a suspect. Raffi is."

"Do you believe he actually ...?"

"No, of course not," I said. "But I have a bad feeling about the whole thing."

Jon put his hand on mine. "Why?" he said.

"I wish I knew."

"I met Jon's parents," I said.

"And?" Mom's mouth was full of cornbread, but she asked anyway.

"They're nice. They read a lot. Mrs. Bell paints."

"Speaking of reading," Mom said, "there was an article on vegetarianism I wanted to save but I can't find the magazine. Have either of you seen it?"

I shrugged.

"I think I read it," Raffi said. "But I don't know where. Is Jon's mother Abby Bell, Jess?"

I shrugged again.

"You saw paintings?"

I nodded.

"Abstracts? Lots of colour? Geometric shapes flowing into each other?" he asked.

"Yeah," I said. "How did you know?"

"She's a real artist," he said. "I knew she lived around here somewhere. So when do we get to meet Jon?"

"I dunno," I said. "What's going on here?"

"Sheena called," Mom said. "She wants to see you tomorrow, after school. She'll pick you up out front unless she hears from you."

"Maybe Jon will come too," I said.

Mom cut herself a second piece of cornbread. "You aren't spending much time with Kelly these days. Is anything wrong?"

"Is that a way of saying I shouldn't spend so much time with Jon?"

"No. Not at all. Don't be so quick to criticize, Jess. I just don't want you to lose Kelly because of some guy."

"He isn't just some guy! And it's Kelly who hasn't got time for me, not the other way around."

Mom's eyes and mine met, and held.

"She's very involved with Joey," I said. "And she hasn't been making it to school that much." Kelly would be really upset if she knew I'd said that. Too bad.

CHAPTER 16

The cruiser was waiting in front of the school. Sheena popped the lock on the passenger door as Jon and I crossed the sidewalk.

"OK if I bring a friend?" I said.

She shook her head. "Sorry. This is an official interview." This was the bullet-word Sheena, not the friendly one. I turned to Jon and raised one corner of my mouth. "See you tomorrow," I said.

Sheena pulled a U-turn on Jameson, and headed back towards King Street. "I thought we'd just cruise around a bit." she said. "Rather than go to the station."

"Sure. Is something wrong?"

"It'll keep," she said.

We followed the Lakeshore to the Exhibition grounds, which were almost deserted. The lake was grey, and the sky was covered by a dirty-looking blanket of clouds.

"It's about Raffi," she said.

I kept looking at the lake. "What about him?"

"How long has he been hanging around with your mom?"

"I was eleven," I said. "Four years. A little more."

"I was reading over your statement this morning..."

I sighed. It was almost a relief to know what was coming.

"And you were a little, uh, cute, weren't you?" she said.

"Cute?" Sitting in the front seat of the cruiser meant I didn't have to look at her, which was fine with me. She was looking at me though, I could see her out of the corner of my left eye.

"*It's just Mom and me.* That's what you said."

"That Bud guy asked me who lived with us. I told the truth."

"You implied that your mom was alone. That she didn't have anybody."

I turned to her then. "He didn't need to be so insulting! Even you saw that. Remember how you pretended to shoot him?"

Sheena shook her head. "I didn't tell you to lie! A cop can ask you anything he darn well wants, so long as it's relevant to what he's investigating. What interests me is why you were covering up for this guy."

"Covering up?"

"Pretending he didn't exist."

I sighed again. "One of his friends, another black guy, who hadn't done anything bad at all, got shot by a cop just two days before! Raffi worries about things like that. The police scare him."

"I noticed. People can be scared of cops for lots of different reasons, I guess, but the most common one is that they've done something against the law."

"I didn't lie," I said.

"You misled the police," she said.

"What does it matter whether my mother has a boyfriend or not? What's that got to do with anything?"

"Don't play smart games, Jess."

Another car pulled into the lot, circled around, then left. Sheena tapped her fingers on the steering wheel, like she was really irritated. She probably was. I swallowed hard.

"If you were me," she said, "dealing with you, a witness to a crime, a witness who covered up for someone, what would you think?"

When I didn't answer, she did.

"You'd be suspicious about why," she said.

"I told you why."

"And you'd wonder about the other stuff this witness told you. Whether it's reliable. Whether the witness is covering up something else."

"I'm not covering up anything! The Orellanas heard the same stuff I did!"

"That's true, they did. But they weren't able to identify either male voice. You said one was Mr. Bird, but you didn't know the other."

"That's true!"

"So now I'm wondering if you were covering up again. When you said you couldn't identify that second voice."

I shook my head. "I never heard the other guy before in my life."

"We have a report that someone who could have been Raffi was there that night. That he came around from the back of your building. At about 3:00 A.M."

"Who? Who said that?"

"A neighbour."

"That person's lying!"

"What makes you so sure? Raffi left work at twelve, and he usually stays till two."

I swallowed again. "Raffi isn't a murderer! I know him. He's kind, and gentle. I've never even heard him raise his voice!"

"Is he a druggie?"

"Raffi? No! He hardly even drinks!"

"The guy this witness saw was big. The guy you saw when he broke in that night you were babysitting was big. Raffi's big."

I groaned. "So is half the world! And the man I saw wasn't Raffi."

"I thought you couldn't identify him? Couldn't see enough."

"I couldn't, but if he was someone I knew, I'm sure I'd have..."

"He made some kind of noise, in the baby's room. So you heard his voice ..."

"It wasn't Raffi! And I think it was sort of a laugh," I said. "But it didn't have any voice sound to it. It was like he let out his breath."

"A laugh? The murderer comes back to the scene of the crime, scares the living daylights out of you, and then laughs? And you think he wasn't someone you know?"

I had nothing to say to that, so that's what I said. Nothing.

When my mother gets mad she paces and waves her hands around. Fortunately, she was mad at Sheena, not me, but I felt guilty anyhow.

"Can she do that?" she said. "Question Jess like that, without an adult present?"

Raffi shrugged.

So did I. "She did it," I said.

"Cooped up in a cop car!" Mom said. "Confined! Like you were in jail!"

"It wasn't that bad. I mean she didn't lock me in or anything," I said. "At least I don't think she did."

Raffi wasn't too happy either, but for a different reason. "I don't like the way this is developing," he said. "Do you think I'm a suspect?"

"Don't be ridiculous, Raffi," Mom said. "I should complain, that's what I should do. She's not going to get away with treating Jess like that." She opened the fridge, poked around for a while, then shut it. "Who is it you report things like that to? The Police Complaints Commission, isn't it?"

"Mom..."

Raffi held up his hand, warning me off. "You'll only make things worse, Lynda," he said. "Just draw more attention to me. Make that cop even madder."

"But you haven't done anything!" Mom wailed.

"It's my fault," I said. When nobody disagreed with me, I got up and started setting the table for supper. Raffi had cooked: soup from a can and grilled cheese sandwiches.

I looked over at Mom. "You can't complain," I said. "Sheena phoned you. You knew she was going to talk to me."

Mom looked like she didn't want to agree, but eventually she nodded. "I suppose," she said. "I could have said I wanted to be there. I could have protected you better."

"Let it drop, Lynda," Raffi said. Then he turned to me. "Run what that cop said by me again, Jess. The stuff about the witness."

"Somebody, probably Mr. Orellana, says he saw a big guy leave here at about three o'clock that night, a big guy who came from behind the building. The other thing is, Sheena thinks I'm lying about the night of the murder. She thinks I did recognize that second man's voice."

"Supposed to be me, I guess." Raffi looked at the floor for a while. "I don't feel too good," he said.

Mom moved to the arm of his chair, and started patting his head. I picked up my backpack and headed down the hall. I can't stand mush.

"Sheena has a witness," I said. "And she says this witness saw some big guy leave here the night of the murder. So she's decided it was Raffi, because he's big." I was on the phone, the extension in my room, talking to Jon.

"Are you sure it wasn't?" he said.

"Jon! There are other big men!"

"Look, don't get me wrong here," he said. "I'm just throwing out ideas. But I have this theory. Are you going to bite my head off if you don't like it?"

"I don't know. It depends on what you say."

"What if... What if Raffi is Tammi's boyfriend? I mean, that wouldn't necessarily mean he's the murderer, but ..."

I closed my eyes. "I don't need this!" I said. "Raffi is my mother's boyfriend. He *loves* her! There is no way he's involved with Tammi!"

"And if you're wrong, Jess? What then? You could be in danger."

"I'm not wrong. I can't be wrong," I added.

CHAPTER 17

I had some stuff to work out in my head, so I was glad when Mom and Raffi left for work. Mom doesn't like it when I just sit around and think. *Staring into space*, she calls it.

She's also not too keen on the fact that I like to be alone, or I did, before the murder. Since then, I haven't been quite so enthusiastic. Old buildings creak and groan a lot, especially at night. The sounds they make remind me of things I'd rather forget, like strangers creeping around the halls, and footsteps on the back stairs.

As soon as Mom was out the door, I headed for my room. When I told Sheena it wasn't Raffi in Tammi's apartment, I meant it. Later, after I talked to Jon, I began to wonder. What if I was wrong?

I clicked open my binder, took out a piece of lined paper, and put it on the desk in front of me. Then I wrote WHO WAS THE MAN IN TAMMI'S APARTMENT? across the top.

My window looks out on the brick wall of the house beside us, so I lowered the blind. It's a nice cranberry colour, one of those fabric things with cords that move it up and down in big folds. I sat looking at it for a while. Then I went out to the kitchen, got an apple, washed it, and came back.

The only time I really saw the man was at the window in Tammi's back door. He was just a shadow, a profile, wearing a peaked cap, the kind a ball-player wears. Raffi didn't even own a hat like that, or if he did, I never saw it. He had a black knit thing he wore in the winter, pulled down over his ears, but I never saw him in a ball cap.

I took a big bite from the apple. Raffi's hair was short. After he shaved it off a couple of months ago, he let it grow back, but just a little, just enough to satisfy Mom. I closed my eyes, trying to picture the guy at the door that night. Did his hair show? I didn't remember any, but that didn't mean anything. Lots of guys shave their heads.

What else? A hand on the window. Fingers tapping like a drum; one-two-three-four, one-two-three-four, one after the other. A man's hand; it could have been black or it could have been white. In the shadows, it was impossible to tell.

When the hand poked through the glass, it was wrapped in something. A jacket? It was something heavy, maybe wool, or fleece. Raffi didn't have jackets like that. He had a leather one, and a windbreaker. It was some light waterproof material; green, with a purple-and-white band across the middle.

What happened next? The hand reached down towards the lock. I think he pulled his arm back, then put it through again. He probably pulled the jacket off, he couldn't have turned the bolt with his fingers covered, but I wasn't getting a replay. Nothing came.

I couldn't sit still any more so I got up and moved around my room. All this hard work wasn't getting me anywhere at all. I never even saw the man again, because after he put his arm through the window, Flavia and I took off down the hall. Was that it? Was that all I knew about him? It couldn't be; I didn't see him again, but I certainly heard him. I knew exactly where he was the whole time he was in the apartment. I knew from his light, and from the sounds he made when he moved around.

Footsteps, that's what came next. If you know people well enough you can tell who they are by the way they walk. I could tell the difference between Mom and Raffi coming up the stairs, or even between Mom and Tammi. I wouldn't necessarily know who Tammi was, I'd only know she wasn't Mom. Unfortunately, about all I remembered about the footsteps was how terrified I was when they were coming towards me, and how relieved I was when they were going away. Maybe that was good. Maybe if it was Raffi up there, I would have known.

But it wasn't the footsteps that came next. What came next was the laugh. That came after he turned the flashlight off, or maybe even just before. It wasn't a ho-ho kind of a laugh, it was a whispery sound, the kind you'd make if you were surprised, if something silly had happened.

I tried out a few whispery laughs myself, trying to make them sound like his. "Ssss," I said. I practised a bit, pushing the sound out of my mouth, but I wasn't getting it quite right. There was something missing. I ran through the alphabet in my head, like I was playing that hangman game, where you know some letters of a word and have to figure out the rest. "Asss, Bsss, Csss, Dsss, Esss," I said. That sounded better, but I kept going. "Fsss, Gsss, Hsss," I said. "Isss, Jsss."

My name, was that what I heard? *Jess*, sort of hissing out of his mouth, like he was totally shocked to see me there? My name, from the mouth of the killer!

I stared at my blind for a while, thinking how much that cranberry colour reminded me of blood. Then I put my thick fleecy housecoat on over my clothes, because I was freezing.

Maybe I was mistaken, maybe that's not what I heard at all. I played with that idea for a while, but I knew it wasn't true. It's pretty hard to mistake your own name. What was so amazing was that I didn't clue in before, that I sort of heard what he said at the time, but I didn't remember it until now.

I shivered, because there was something else. Something worse. If the killer knew me, then I knew the killer.

The phone was right in front of me. I looked at it, I even put my hand on it, but who could I call? Who could I tell?

Sheena, who was ready to nail Raffi already?

Mom, who'd fall apart?

Kelly, who wouldn't be at home, or even care?

I could call Jon, or Flavia, but I knew what they'd say. They'd tell me to call Sheena, because they'd be scared I'd get hurt, because I knew too much.

I didn't even want to think about that, so I didn't. Instead, I took a very long, very hot shower. Then I went to bed and pulled the covers over my head.

CHAPTER 18

Stomping around the apartment the next morning, getting myself organized for school, I made a list in my head of all the people I knew who were big and who had anything at all to do with the Birds. There weren't many. Ray himself was big, but he was dead. Sheena was big too, but she was a cop. Jon was tall but not what I'd call big, and anyhow he didn't come on the scene until after the murder. Then there was Raffi. The list was useless.

By this time I was ready to get dressed, so I did what I do every morning. I put on some clothes; then I looked in the mirror. It wasn't a pretty sight. "Wonderful," I said. "Good work, Jess."

Mom, just home from work, popped down the hall to see if I was still alive. "Talking to yourself is a bad sign," she said. Then she looked at me and giggled. "Bad hair day?"

"Grotesque," I said.

"Don't tell me, let me guess. You went to bed with it wet?"

"Um," I said.

"Maybe you should start over. Stick your head under the tap, then blow it dry."

"Thank you for that kind suggestion." I probably didn't sound too friendly.

"A bit grumpy, are we? Hormones giving you trouble?"

I made a blowing out, ticked-off sort of noise, and left the room, shutting the door firmly behind me, so firmly that the frame vibrated.

When Mom is mad, her voice really carries. "Jess!" she yelled. "Get back in here!"

I got back in there.

"I know you're upset," she said. "But still..."

"Sorry." I blinked twice, then I threw my arms around her neck and bawled.

It poured rain all day. At school, I spoke only when I was spoken to, and then as little as possible. After my last class I found a message from the principal taped to my locker. Mrs. Carelli would like to see me as soon as possible, it said.

The office was pretty full and there weren't any seats left, so after I told the secretary why I was there, I leaned against the wall and looked around. Most of the kids were there to explain absences, past or future, and most of the absences were for pretty ordinary reasons. They were sick or they had to look after their kid sister, or go to the dentist, or to somebody's funeral. One guy said that the train coming back from Kitchener broke down, but he didn't say why he was in Kitchener on a school day. Another, who was wearing a little Band-Aid on his forehead, said he'd been in a car accident. The best excuse was the nose-bleed that wouldn't stop. The worst was the washing machine that broke down with all the girl's clothes in it, soaking wet.

Mrs. Carelli came to the door of the inner office, wagged her finger at me and smiled, which was nice of her, because it was like telling everybody watching that I wasn't in trouble. She was wearing a suit like a man's but it had a skirt instead of pants. It was a bluish-grey colour, and when she sat down, she slipped the jacket over the back of her chair, showing a striped blue-and-white blouse underneath.

"I take it Ronny Roach hasn't apologized," she said.

I shook my head.

"Have you had any communication with him at all?"

"Not exactly," I said. "But ..." I leaned my backpack on my leg and dug into it, desperate for something, anything, I could use as a handkerchief.

Mrs. Carelli moved from her chair and handed me a box of tissues, then perched on the front corner of the desk, facing me. "I hope you can tell me about it," she said.

I hoped I could too, without blubbering all over the floor. I put the box on the chair beside me, and did a mop-up job on my nose. "Sorry," I said. "I'm not really a whiner."

"I know you aren't," she said. "Has he done something?"

"It's just the way he..." How do you say that it isn't just the Roach, that it's everything? Maybe you don't. Maybe you just stick to the subject. I snorted into the tissue again before I answered.

"I didn't see him for a while," I said. "And then I did, in the hall. And he looked so mad, so ... absolutely furious. Like he wanted to just kill me." I started shivering all over, just from remembering. "Seriously kill me," I added. "I didn't imagine it. My friend saw it too."

"I didn't realize," she said. "That makes the situation more difficult, doesn't it?"

"He lives on my street," I said.

"I'm aware of that." She tapped her index finger on the desk for a moment. "What I'd normally do at this point is bring him in, ask why there's no apology, and if one wasn't forthcoming, suspend him until he gave it."

Our eyes met, and I gulped.

"Yes," she said. "It's a dilemma, isn't it? If I do that, you're likely to be even more frightened. With some cause, I suspect. But if I don't enforce the policy, it won't take long for word to get around that I'm soft on harassment."

I didn't see what she could do, but at least she understood.

She tapped her finger some more. "Maybe I'll bring him in for a warning. Make sure he understands there can be absolutely no repercussions against you. I'll tell him I've advised you to contact the police if he bothers you. Are you still in touch with Constable Sheena Bowes?"

"Sort of," I said. "But she's mad at me too. I don't think I want to ask for any favours right now."

"Is this something you want to talk about?"

I do, desperately, but it will take a while... I shifted my eyes towards the outer office. There were at least three kids out there waiting to see her.

"I'll make time, Jessica." She smiled. "Just let me speak to my secretary. She can reschedule some of my appointments."

I heard her voice outside the door. When she came back, she was carrying two little bottles of apple juice, one for each of us.

The first sentence was pretty hard to get out, but after that, I just babbled. I told her about Raffi being a suspect without an alibi. I told her how Sheena thought I was covering up for him, and how I was beginning to wonder about that myself, and how bad that made me feel. Then I told her how Sheena'd pretended to be my friend, when all she really wanted was information about the Orellanas. I said I didn't think that was fair, because they were people I liked a lot, who I had to live near, maybe for a long time. The more I talked, the more upset I got. Mrs. Carelli didn't look too pleased either, especially when I told her about being questioned in the police car.

When I finally finished, she let out a long sigh. "You have a serious problem," she said. "Several of them."

For some weird reason that made me feel better.

"What I'd like to do," she said. "Is arrange for some police contact for you, either with Sheena Bowes or with a different officer, one who isn't involved in the murder investigation."

"My second suggestion is that you should request that your mother or some other adult is present if the police want to interview you again. Are you close to your father? He'd be ideal, in this situation."

I couldn't believe what I was hearing! I'd gone for years without anyone even mentioning my father. Now he was coming up in every second conversation! "How do you know about him?" I said.

"He's listed in your school records." she said. "And, of course, I know of his reputation."

"I haven't seen my father since I was twelve."

She looked sad about that, but she didn't say anything, she just nodded. "My third suggestion is that you arrange to walk to and from school with another student, at least for a while. Can you do that?"

I nodded. Flavia would help me, I knew she would. She was a really nice friend.

"Now, about the murder, about not knowing who or what to believe about your friend Raffi, all I can suggest is that you be extremely careful. I realize that you don't want to offend him or your mother with ... suspicions, but your first responsibility is to ensure your own safety." She paused, as if she was thinking about what to say next. "If there is anything I can do, even to the extent of consulting your father on your behalf, I'd be glad to do that."

"No!" I said. "Please don't."

"Without your permission, of course I won't. But I am available myself, at any time. And I'm sure Constable Bowes is too. She may be annoyed with you, but I'm absolutely certain she wouldn't let that stop her if you had difficulties with ... personal safety. Do you understand what I'm saying?"

"I understand," I said.

CHAPTER 19

When I came in the door from school my mother was holding the phone away from her, like it smelled bad. "It's Sheena," she whispered.

I gave my nostrils a quick pinch and put the receiver to my ear. "Hi," I said.

"Hi, duckie. I hear you're mad at me."

"Did my mother tell you that?" I frowned at Mom across the room. She put her hands up in front of her, palms out, and shook her head.

"Your mother was somewhat frosty," Sheena said. "Is she mad too?"

"You've been talking to Mrs. Carelli," I said.

"Yep. She chewed me out, if it's any consolation. So I phoned to explain. If I can," she said. "If you'll listen."

I didn't say anything, but I was sure thinking. Mostly about Mrs. Carelli shooting her mouth off. For my own good, of course.

"You thought I was a friend," Sheena said. "Now you think I wasn't. I was just pretending, right?"

I didn't answer.

She sighed. "You aren't making this easy, you know."

I didn't say anything to that either.

"Did anybody ever tell you that your silences would stop a train?"

"No," I said.

"Look, I'm a cop and I like people. So we had some fun together. But sometimes the cop part of me has to take over."

I still wasn't saying anything, but I was listening. I guess she knew, because she didn't stop talking.

"Being a cop has to come first. I mean that's how we met, right. You know what I am."

"Yeah," I said.

"So I should always act like a cop? If I like someone, I should hide it?"

"Probably."

"Well, maybe you're right. It would sure be a lot easier than trying to communicate with one really ticked-off person. Sweating to try and make her understand."

"I think you're trying to talk to me because you need my help again," I said. "Or maybe you got worried because Mrs. Carelli knows how you treated me."

Mom was sitting at the table, facing away from me, pretending to read the paper. I knew she was listening because her right fist shot up, and her thumb was raised high above that.

"That wasn't nice, Jess," Sheena said. "Not nice at all."

It was just as well she couldn't see my grin. "So I'm not perfect," I said.

"Well, look. I guess I'm not making much headway here. But I didn't call for information. I called because I felt bad. My job took over, but it has to sometimes."

"OK."

"I'm not apologizing. I'm just explaining. Right?"

"Yeah."

"So how are you doing?"

"Not so good."

"Wanna talk about it?"

I hesitated. I didn't, but I might need her if the Roach got any uglier. "Yeah," I said. "I guess." My voice sounded like I was ten years old. "Remember how I told you there was some guy hassling me?"

"Sure. I was gonna shake him up a bit, but you weren't too keen on that."

"Yeah. Well, I reported him to the principal. And now he's in trouble at school, and ..."

"The offer's still open," she said. "Just let me know, and I'll do what I can."

"OK," I said. I was just going to explain about the Roach, about how scary he is, when she changed the subject.

"Before I forget," she said. "Does the name Al Green mean anything to you?"

"I thought you just called because you felt bad," I said. "You didn't want any more information. But no, it doesn't. Who's Al Green?"

"Someone real close to Mrs. Bird. A kind of neighbour," she said. "And don't be so touchy."

Probably I was being touchy, but there she was, pumping me, up to her old tricks again. I never did get around to telling her any more about Ronny Roach; I never even told her his name. I guess I showed her.

I figured I'd better take Mrs. Carelli's warning seriously, so the next day I had two friends walk me home from school, Flavia and Jon. Neither of them knew anybody called Al Green.

"Who's he?" Jon said.

"Somebody really close to Tammi, according to Sheena." I made quotation marks with my fingers when I said the word *close*. "He's also a neighbour."

"Mrs. Tammi has a close friend?" Flavia said. "Does that mean she has a boyfriend? So soon?"

We were stopped at a corner, waiting to cross. Jon and I shrugged at the same time.

"If he lives around here," Jon said, "we could try to find him."

"The cops must have done that already," I said.

Flavia looked thoughtful. "We could look also. It is possible that people would tell us things they would not tell the police."

"Sure," Jon said. "We could go door to door. Ask people if they know him. Check out names on mailboxes."

"OK," I said. "Let's do it."

Our block has fourteen houses that are chopped up into apartments, one duplex, one triplex (ours), a ten-unit building, a twelve-unit building (where Raffi lives) and at the far end of the street, an old-age home.

The mail boxes were brass-coloured wall units, with slots holding name cards and individual keyholes. It took over an hour to cover the whole block, but a lot of that time we were just fooling around.

We told some of the neighbours that we were doing a survey on front halls. We told others that we were counting cats. The neighbours told us about the cop who'd been around asking questions about the night of the murder. Nobody could remember being asked about Al Green.

We graded the halls on a scale of one to ten for cleanliness, smells and security. Our building was a nine and a half, demoted from ten because of a pile of advertising flyers in one corner. The worst was a minus fifteen, which smelled like a drunk had just up-chucked his last meal. Outside, after I'd taken a deep breath, I turned to Jon.

"You know who lives there?" I said.

"Yup. The Roaches. Rotten Ronny and his old man."

We counted between thirteen and fifteen cats: eight grey-striped tabbies; between one and three solid-coloured blacks, depending on how fast they travelled and which of us was counting; two blacks with white markings; one white with black markings, and one very unhappy Siamese caged beside an open window.

We didn't count the kids; but there were dozens of them, from all over the world, playing together. Africans, Central Americans, Vietnamese, Chinese, Indians. Kids from countries I probably never even heard of. We found one family of Browns, but no Greens at all, not even one.

CHAPTER 20

When we left the school Kelly and I turned towards my place, like we had hundreds of times before. Thousands of times, probably — about three days a week since we were in kindergarten.

Kelly was serious today. "I'm really tired of being a kid," she said.

I laughed. "What does that mean? You aren't a kid."

She shook her head, like she couldn't believe how thick I was. "I'm cutting out," she said. "For good."

"You mean you're leaving? You're quitting school?"

"Quitting school and leaving home," she said. "Joey and me, we're going out west."

I grabbed her arm and pulled her onto the grass, away from a horde of students bearing down on us. "Have you told your parents?" I said. It was a dumb question. What could they do? How could they stop her? They'd have to tie her up.

"Not yet," she said. She lifted my hand from her arm and moved back onto the sidewalk.

My head got the message, but my mouth didn't. "I thought you wanted to teach kindergarten."

She shrugged and looked away.

"I'm saying such dumb things," I said. "Do you have any money?"

She laughed then, the old Kelly laugh, a wheezing giggle. "Thirteen dollars," she said. "Joey has a brother in Vancouver. We can crash at his place. For a while, anyway."

I slid my backpack to the sidewalk, pulled out my emergency ten-dollar bill and tucked it into her shirt pocket. "Will you write?"

"Sure," she said. "Well ..." She grinned her kindergarten grin, turned and walked away from me.

I didn't even get to say goodbye. I didn't even hug her. I just stood there on the corner, watching her until she was out of sight.

When I got home, Mom was in the shower. Parents stick together. If she found out, she'd be on the phone to Kelly's mother before I could blink.

When the shower stopped, I knocked on the bathroom door. "I'm home," I said. "I have a headache. I'm going to have a nap."

"Are you getting a cold?" she asked. "You sound funny."

"Probably," I said.

Two days later Mrs. Curran phoned Mom. I got blasted as I walked in the door.

"Did you know Kelly was leaving?" she said. Like a lot of the stuff Mom says, there was more there than the actual words. *If you knew and didn't say anything, you're in big trouble.*

There was no point in lying, she wouldn't believe me. "Sort of," I said.

"That's why you've been so quiet, isn't it? Moping in your room? Drooping like some wilted flower?"

I nodded.

"I don't suppose it occurred to you that you had an obligation to tell her parents about this?"

I buttoned my lips together and looked at the floor. It had occurred to me. The obligation to keep my former best friend's secret had occurred to me too, and that obligation won. There wasn't much to say, so I just shrugged.

"Mrs. Curran wants to talk to you. She's in a real snit, and I don't blame her, so you'd better get yourself over there right away," she said.

"Do I have to?" I looked at the floor again. "If she feels any worse than I do, I'm really sorry for her," I said.

Mom put her hand on the back of my head. She even cried a little. "It's the least you can do," she said. "And if you know anything, tell her."

I was just heading out the door, when she called me back. "Jess! Remember what Mrs. Carelli said. Ask Flavia to go with you."

Mrs. Curran hugged me, and I hugged her back, but I didn't like the way she looked at Flavia, as if there was something wrong with her being there, something wrong with me having a new friend.

The Pain was doing little jumps all around us, hopping with both feet at the same time. She made me tired to look at her. Then she started chanting: "Kelly split, Kelly split, Kelly is a stupid twit."

"Enough, Melissa. Quiet down, or go upstairs!" Mrs. Curran took her apron off and, still carrying it, ushered us into their front room. I didn't take this as a good sign.

"Jessica, I'm going to take it for granted that you knew exactly what was going on," she said.

"Well, not exactly," I said. "I mean, I really didn't know exactly." I sounded pitiful even to myself, but I never thought this was going to be easy. "When did she leave?" I said.

"You don't know?"

"No. She told me she was going, but she didn't say when."

Mrs. Curran wiped at her eyes with the corner of her apron. "Sometime yesterday afternoon. I'd just dropped over to the store, to pick up a few things for dinner. Nothing I couldn't have done without..."

"Do you know where they went?"

She shook her head. "Her dad's over at the Montes' now, talking to them, seeing if Joey left any messages, but it's not likely, is it?"

"She told me they were going out west, to Joey's brother's," I said. "In Vancouver."

Mrs. Curran frowned. "As far as I know," she said, "the only brother Joey has is seven years old."

When Mrs. Curran bustled to the phone, the Pain entertained us by doing backwards somersaults on the living-room floor, with commentary. "You really fell for that one, didn't you, Jess?"

"Maybe he has another brother," I said.

But he didn't. No sisters either. It was a false trail, and what bugged me most, was that Kelly got me to lay it.

CHAPTER 21

Jon's hand felt sweaty in the heat, and our bare arms brushed against each other. I always thought hanging onto a guy in public was sort of tacky, but that was before I had anybody to hang onto.

We were crossing the pedestrian bridge to get to the lake. "I have a whole lot of stuff to tell you," I said. I was practically running to keep up with him. "Could you slow down or take smaller steps or something?"

"Sure," he said.

The lake was a deep blue satin, rippled by the wind, and seemed to go on forever. Sailboats from the marinas along the shore flashed in the sunlight. We sat on an uncomfortable slatted bench; Jon stretched his legs out in front of him, then he turned to me and smiled. "You know more about the murder?"

I nodded. "You know the man in Tammi's apartment that night?" I said. "Well, I remembered something about him. Something important." I looked at the sky, then I looked back at Jon again. "He knew me. He actually said my name, like he was surprised to see me there."

"Oh-oh," Jon said. "Raffi?"

That was the one question I didn't want to answer, or even think about, but I couldn't put it off any longer. "I don't think so," I said. "At least I didn't *recognize* Raffi, not at all. Not one thing reminded me of him. But who else could it be?"

Jon's arm slid along the back of the bench behind me, as if it was moving without any connection to his brain. "Who knew you were babysitting that night?" he said.

"Mom. All the Orellana family. And Tammi, of course. Why?"

"What about Raffi? Did he know?"

"Yeah."

"So why do you think it would be him? Why would he be surprised...?"

I flung myself back on the bench and threw my arms to the sky. "He wouldn't! He wouldn't have been surprised! It *couldn't* have been Raffi! Oh, I'm so happy! Thank you, Jon, thank you! You're brilliant, absolutely brilliant."

His whole face was grinning. "What can I say?" he said. "Brilliant is probably a *slight* exaggeration, but ..."

"I can't believe I didn't think of that," I said. I stared at the lake for a while longer, then I twisted my fingers together, hard.

Jon rested his hand on my wrist. "What's going on?" he said. "All of a sudden you tensed right up. I won't bite, I promise."

I sighed. "It makes me feel better to know it wasn't Raffi, a whole lot better, but the cops still suspect him. He had to go to the police station today, to be in some line-up."

"Maybe it's not important," Jon said. He didn't really think that, I could tell. He was just trying to make me feel better.

"There's something else, too," I said. "I don't want to tell Sheena."

"That the guy knew you?"

I nodded.

"Because she'll think it was Raffi?"

"Yeah. But if I don't tell her, I'm in trouble. She was talking about ...*withholding information*. Like it was a crime or something. I don't want to go to jail!"

"Maybe we should ask somebody about that. A lawyer."

"My father's a lawyer," I said.

"He is? Well, why don't you call him?"

"No," I said. "I'd feel too stupid. I haven't seen him for three years. More than that, actually."

"If you don't do it soon, you never will," Jon said. "And right now you've got a really good reason..."

"I can't," I said. The waves were bigger now because the wind was stronger. Two sailboats were lying on their sides in the water, and a third tipped over as I watched. Somebody in a power boat was busy rescuing everybody.

"Why did you stop seeing him?" Jon said.

The sky was robin's-egg blue, with some wisps of cotton-wool clouds whipping around. "I'm not sure," I said. "He and Mom had this big fight, and after that she got all upset whenever he came to get me. So I got upset too. Then one day she told me I didn't *have* to see him if I didn't want to." I was quiet for a while, thinking. "I was just a kid," I said. "I didn't want her to be unhappy."

"If you see him now, will she get unhappy again?"

"I don't know," I said. "Probably. She never wants to talk about him. Even though ..."

"What?"

"He's ...on the news a lot, on TV. And in the papers."

"You're kidding! What's his name?"

"Gordon March."

"Gordon March is your father! He's almost famous."

"I know," I said. "Why would he want to be bothered with me?"

It was eight o'clock at night, and Raffi hadn't come back from being in the line-up. I was in my room, flipping through my math text, trying to convince myself I was learning something. Mom was at work.

When the phone rang, I jumped. "They did it," Mom said. Her voice was small, like a little kid's. I could hardly hear her. "They arrested Raffi. For the murder."

"No!"

"Yes," she whispered.

We were both quiet for a while. "Do you think he did it?" I'd never asked her that before, but it seemed like a good time for it.

She didn't answer, but I heard a small sniff.

"What's that supposed to mean?" I asked.

"I don't know. I can't believe he did, but ..." She left the sentence dangling in the air, which is something she does a lot. I'm supposed to read her mind, I guess.

"But what?"

"The cops have a witness who saw him leave the building that night."

"That's just Mr. Orellana," I said. "He saw some big guy come from around the back, that's all."

"No, this is someone else, some guy who identified him from a line-up. Raffi didn't see him, but it wasn't Mr. Orellana, this person knew his name."

"Oh," I said.

She sighed. "It gets worse, Jess. His fingerprints were in Tammi's apartment."

"No. That can't be true. I don't believe it." I didn't, but I had this terrible sinking feeling, as if I was under water, and somebody was pushing me down.

"He'd hardly make it up," Mom said. "Listen, I can't leave here yet, there's no other supervisor to cover for me. I'm still looking for someone, but..."

"What else did Raffi say?" I asked.

"Nothing. Some cop was right on top of him, hurrying him up."

"Does he have a lawyer?"

I could hear her sniffing again. Then I heard the soft scuffing sound a tissue makes when you pull it from the box. "I never even thought of that. We'll have to get him one."

"We?" I said. "I don't like the sound of that *we*."

"You," she said. "He's your father."

"Oh no you don't! I'm just the kid here!"

She blew her nose, and I winced. "You have to," she said. "Who else do we know?"

"How come all of a sudden you're dying for me to talk to him, after years of making him sound like some kind of a louse?"

She didn't answer.

"I won't do it," I said. "I'm not that two-faced." Then I stopped talking. Completely.

"I was afraid I'd lose you," she whispered.

"Lose me?" I said. "What are you talking about? You'd forget me on the streetcar?"

"You'd want to live with him."

"Mom! I wouldn't." Then I stopped myself. "He did want me to live with him, didn't he? I'd forgotten all about that. That was what the big fight was about."

I could hardly hear her now. "He has so much money," she said. "And you thought he was so wonderful."

Suddenly, I was furious. "So now I'm supposed to call him? After three years of refusing to talk to him? To ask for a favour?"

"Don't yell," she said. "Everybody on the street will hear you."

I shouted, "I couldn't care less!" Then I crashed the phone down without saying goodbye, something I'd never done before. After that I threw my math book at the wall. I hadn't done that before, either.

CHAPTER 22

Half an hour later I hauled the phone book from its shelf and looked up my father's number. The kid who answered told me I had reached the March residence. Then he wanted to know who I wished to speak to.

"Mr. March," I said.

"Who should I say is calling?" he asked.

"Jess," I said. "Jess March." Then I waited.

My palms slipped on the receiver and my heart thundered under my ribs. Maybe my father wasn't going to come to the phone at all, maybe he'd get the kid to make an excuse. Besides, if he did come, what then? What can you say to someone you haven't seen for three years, and it's your fault, and you're only calling because your mother made you?

"Jess? Is it really you?" My dad's voice sounded like it was his birthday, and I'd just given him the best present of his whole life.

"It's me," I said.

"You couldn't know how happy I am to hear from you!"

"Me too, I said. My voice got a little fractured then, but maybe he'd think I had a cold. "I'm happy too. I wish I'd phoned before."

"It's a tough spot to be in, between two parents."

"Yeah," I said.

"So, when can I see you? Soon, I hope."

"I need help," I said.

"Do you want me to come and get you?"

"I don't know." Then I said the most perfect thing, and I didn't even plan it. What was so amazing was that I didn't even know it was true until the words popped right out of my mouth. "I think about you all the time," I said. "I mean, I'm calling because I want something, but ..."

"You couldn't say anything nicer than that," he said. "Now, what's the problem?"

I told him everything.

My father's office used to be on Bay Street near the Old City Hall, but he'd moved. Now he was up near Yorkville, but it wasn't hard to find. Two days after we talked on the phone, a Saturday, I took the Queen streetcar as far as University, transferred to the subway, got off at the museum and walked.

The street was in an area where people used to live. The houses were still there, but almost all of them had been turned into fancy restaurants, or art galleries, or offices.

My father's building had big new windows where there had probably been smaller ones and there was a whole lot of wood on the outside that looked unpainted, only it was shiny. The brass sign beside the door said *Gordon March* on one line, and *Barrister* underneath it. Underneath that there was a little white button and a sign that said *Push Bell for Admittance*. When I lifted my hand towards it the door flung open and I was squashed in a huge hug and half lifted, half danced inside.

My father held me away from him and looked me over, but it was such a nice look that I didn't mind at all.

"You are the spitting image, the spitting image," he said, "of my favourite sister, Vera. You remember Vera? She's the gorgeous one."

"You're the spitting image of my dad," I said.

My eyes were watering, but just a little. "Allergy season," I said.

"Runs in the family." He blew his nose on a big white handkerchief, and I laughed because he honked just like a Canada goose going north, just like he always did. "Some things never change," he said. "C'mon and see my great new place!"

The first floor had a waiting room for clients, secretaries' desks loaded with computer stuff, a whole wall of big grey filing cabinets, a big photocopier in its own little room, and a kitchen that was bigger than ours at home. On the second floor there was a bathroom with an old-fashioned tub, now full of plants; a room Dad called his "conference room-slash-library"; and in the front, looking out over the street, his private office.

A chocolate-brown leather couch and some matching chairs were grouped around a coffee table at one end of the room, and at the other there was a wooden desk so shiny you could see yourself in it. Two pictures in matching stand-up frames faced where Dad sat. The one of me was so old, I was still wearing a pony tail. In the other one a blonde woman sat with her arm around a boy.

"My wife," Dad said. "And her son, from her first marriage."

Just to be polite, I had another look. The kid looked like trouble.

There was one file folder, a bright red one, lying on the desk. Dad picked it up and settled in his chair. "How about we talk business first," he said. "Then after that, we'll talk about ourselves. Maybe get some lunch. Deal?"

I squeezed my hands together. "Deal," I said.

"I spent about an hour with Raffi yesterday. And after that I spoke to the Crown Attorney. She has a file like this with all the police evidence in it, and she's the one who'll be against us in court."

He sighed, and looked across at me. His face was sort of sad. "I hope you aren't expecting miracles," he said. "I can't wave a magic wand and get him released."

He was watching me, which was something he'd been doing a lot of ever since I got there. Finally I said, "You think he did it, don't you?"

He hesitated. "That's an impossible question to answer right now."

"You think he did it, and you don't want to tell me." I said. "Because you know I'll be really upset."

"What's important Jess, is what the police and the Crown Attorney think. Let me tell you about the evidence against him. Perhaps between us we can find some flaws in it."

"OK" I wiped a tear away with my thumb. He saw that too.

"First, there are the two eyewitnesses," he said. "People who independently saw someone leave your building that night."

"Mr. Orellana is one," I said. "But he only said it was someone big."

"Here we are. Statement of Roberto Orellana. I'll read it. *The person I saw was big like the black man who visits Mrs. March. He came from around the side of the building. It was three o'clock in the morning.* The other person," Dad said, turning over some more pages, "— where is that statement? — the other witness wasn't able to pinpoint the time, but he saw a man leave the building through the front door some time during the night..."

"Through the front? And the other guy said from the side?"

"Yes. I pointed out that discrepancy to the Crown Attorney, but if she thought it was important, she didn't let on. Anyway, this second witness later identified Raphael Morgan, Raffi, as the person he saw that night. He picked him out of a line-up."

"Who was it who saw him?" I said.

Dad had his finger holding a place in the file, and he turned back to it. "Here we are," he said. The second witness. Ronald Roach. That name sounds familiar."

My mouth dropped open.

"Are you OK, Jess? Is this stuff getting to be too much for you?"

"*Ronald Roach* is too much for me," I said. "Ronald Roach is ..." For a moment I didn't know where to start. I just sat there flapping my hands around. Then I remembered. Dad was there at the beginning.

"You know him," I said. "He cut Natalie's hair off. In front of my school."

"Him!" Dad said. "He's still in the area?"

"He was away for a while but he came back. He's in one of my classes."

Dad frowned. "He was in detention. Then he was supposed to live with some relative up north, if I remember correctly."

"Well, now he's living with his father just down the street from us and he's been giving me a really hard time. He just *hates* me. I had to report him to the principal because he was harassing me, and since then ..." I did a few more hand flaps, and shook my head. The truth is I was totally flipped out, but in a kind of good way, because I was beginning to smell what the Roach had done.

"Start at the beginning," Dad said. "What was he harassing you about?"

So that's what I did. I told him the whole story about that: the fat-girl words, even the worst ones; the hate stare in the hall when I was with Kelly; the trouble the Roach was in at school; how Raffi talked to him; the whole thing. The more I said, the madder Dad got.

"I'd like to punch that little jerk's lights out," Dad said. "I will, too, but I'll do it legally. From what you've said it seems like this is all verifiable, through the principal? How you've felt personally threatened? The whole thing?" he asked.

"Yes, and through Sheena, the cop. I never told her the Roach's name, but she knows I've been harassed."

Dad was looking at the notes he'd taken when I was talking, and bobbing his head up and down. "There are possibilities here, Jess.

Of discrediting this miserable little... Roach as a witness. Which would certainly be very helpful for Raffi. Let me tell you about the other evidence though, before we get too excited here."

I groaned. "The fingerprints?" I said.

"The fingerprints. A lot of unidentified prints were picked up in the Birds' apartment. Yours are certainly among them. But Raffi's were too."

"I can't believe that," I said. "I just can't."

"Fingerprints don't lie, Jess."

"I know. They weren't just on the door frame or something were they? I mean, if he stopped to talk to Tammi...?"

"They were in two different places. Only two. Which is somewhat unusual. The police theory is that he wiped the others away, and just missed these." Dad shrugged.

I sighed. "Where were they?" I didn't know why I was asking that, but it was something to say.

"On an empty soft drink can, which was on the floor in the living area, and on a magazine. Inside the magazine as well as on the cover, as if he'd looked all through it. Which is a rather strange thing for a murderer to do, but I suppose he could have been waiting for Mr. Bird to come home."

Sometimes when I've forgotten something, but I'm almost remembering it, I have this weird feeling. Mom says it's because the forgotten thing is on the tip of my tongue, but that isn't quite right. It's more like it's on the tip of my brain, outside it, just teasing me. I had that feeling then, but that's all it was. A feeling that I should remember something. It didn't go anywhere.

"The police theory," Dad said, "is that Bird and Raffi were involved in some crime together. That's because of Bird's criminal record. He robbed a bank twelve years ago. Did you know about that?"

"Ray was a bank robber?" I said. "That's really creepy."

Dad was looking at the file again. "Um hum," he said. "His finger-prints showed up on the police computer as those of Al Green, so he'd been living under an assumed name. He was in jail for eight years."

"Ray and Al Green were the same person?" I groaned.

"According to this. Let's just check the description." He turned a few pages over. "Was Bird a big heavy guy?"

"Yeah," I said.

"Hair brown, eyes brown, no distinguishing marks?"

"No!" I said. "He had red hair."

When Dad looked up, he was frowning. "How red?" he said. "Dark or bright?"

"Dark, I guess."

"Funny. Could be some cop is colour-blind," he said. "Hang on a minute." He flipped through some more pages. "Here," he said. "Identification of body: Mrs. Tammi Bird and Mrs. Theresa Goodwin. Do you know this Goodwin woman?"

"Tammi's friend," I said.

"Mmmm." He wrote something down. "Has there been a funeral yet?"

"Last week," I said. "We didn't know about it until it was all over. It was private."

"One last thing. Then we'll go for lunch and a chat. "If the police want to interview you again, I want to know about it."

I nodded. "OK."

"You're in a bit of a bind. They'll be wanting information from you, and if you give them any, they'll use it against Raffi."

"Against Raffi?"

"I'm afraid so. If you're contacted again, don't even tell them the time of day. Just call me."

"Sure," I said.

"You're looking pretty flat, Jess. The giant sit on you again?"

"Yeah," I said. It was an old joke between us, but that's exactly how I felt. The giant sat on me.

CHAPTER 23

After I left my dad, I felt great about him, but terrible about Raffi. It was like I was split into two pieces. When I got home, I knew Mom wouldn't be back from work yet, so I knocked at the Orellanas' door, hoping Flavia would be there, but nobody answered.

Upstairs, when I turned the key in the lock like I usually do, the same key I've been using since I was seven, nothing happened. I had to turn it again before the door would open. I stood out in the hall a moment, thinking about that. Obviously the door hadn't been locked at all. I frowned. Mom left before I did, so I couldn't blame it on her, and Raffi was in jail, so it wasn't him either. Had I done that?

There was another puzzle inside the apartment. A bag of oatmeal cookies, surrounded by crumbs, sat on the table beside an open carton of milk and a used glass. Either we'd had a hungry burglar or someone who knew where we kept the extra key had come by for a snack. I looked around the room. Nothing was missing, and nothing was out of place. It hadn't been a burglar. I thought about the hidden key, and the only other person who knew where we kept it. Then I laughed.

The door to my room was shut. I pushed it open, slowly, shoving aside a dusty green backpack and a pair of wet-looking running shoes. A large lump was huddled under the covers of my bed. The lump had light blonde hair.

I backed carefully out the door, then tiptoed down the hall to the living room and telephoned the lump's mother.

The Pain answered. She was chewing something that snapped. From the sound effects it had to be gum, a big wad of it. Bubble gum.

"This is Jess," I said. "Is your mom there?"

"What do you want her for?"

I groaned. "I need to speak to her," I said. "You shouldn't talk on the phone and blow bubbles at the same time."

"Why?"

"It's rude, you clown."

"I mean why do you want to talk to her, dummy."

"It's important! Just get her, will you. Please?"

"Not until you tell me why you want her, I won't."

I sighed. "If I had a sister like you," I said, "I'd seriously consider running away from home."

"Oink," she said.

I sighed again. "I know where Kelly is," I said.

The phone clattered when she dropped it, and I could hear her screeching. "Mom! Mom! Mom! Guess what? Jess found Kelly!"

Mrs. Curran had a carrying sort of a voice too. "Oh, my goodness! Oh, my dear! Oh, heavens!" I heard. When she picked up the receiver she was doing that laughing-crying thing mothers do when they're really happy. "Jess, dear, is it really true? You got a letter, didn't you? Is she all right? You have absolutely no idea how worried I've been. She did go out west, didn't she? Or was it the States?"

"She's in my bed," I said. "Why don't you come right over?"

After I hung up I went back down the hall to my room, only this time I didn't bother being quiet. I shoved Kelly's things into a corner, pulled the chair away from my desk, and sat down, facing her.

"Somebody's been sleeping in my bed," I said, in a great big Daddy Bear voice. My Momma Bear voice was smooth and refined. Baby Bear squeaked. I was just finishing up with his "Somebody's been sleeping in my bed, and here she is!" when the lump heaved and one bleary blue eye peered out at me.

"Very funny," Kelly mumbled.

"I thought so," I said. "I see you remembered about the key in the flower-pot."

"Um." She pulled herself up on one elbow, and flashed me her kindergarten grin.

"You feel like talking?" I asked.

She combed her hair with her fingers while she thought about that. Then she shrugged and looked at the ceiling. "I got hungry. Joey and I fought. His feet stink."

"I called your mom," I said. "She'll be here in about two minutes."

Kelly looked right at me then. "You didn't."

"I did," I said. Then I flashed *my* kindergarten grin.

"She'll kill me!"

"Nah," I said. "Maybe later, but not in front of me."

Kelly's reunion with her mother was tense. After they left, I changed into shorts and a tank top and headed out to our back deck to work on my tan. I had just finished oiling my legs when I heard noises below me. Somebody was on Tammi's deck too.

I tiptoed across to the stairs, carefully lowered myself onto my stomach and inched my head over the edge. The back part of each step is open, perfect for spying.

It was Tammi. She was all dolled up in hot-pink tights and a matching halter that was barely decent. When she unfolded the stroller and manoeuvred it from the deck into the apartment, I figured that if she was going to walk somewhere, I might learn something if I went too.

As soon as the lock clicked on her back door, I whipped inside, changed into a T-shirt, ran a comb through my hair and grabbed my knapsack. Then I took up a surveillance position at our front window.

Tammi moves fast, even in the killer heels she wears, and it didn't take her long to get Brianna and herself out the front door. When she turned the corner and was out of my view, I ran down the stairs and followed, keeping at least a half block behind her until she turned onto Queen. It's one of the busiest streets in Parkdale, and there are a lot of pedestrians to hide behind, so I moved up a little closer. A few blocks later she turned into a store. I hung back at first, waiting for her to come out, then I jay-walked across the street to get a better view. When I saw the sign I grinned all over my face. Trevor's Travel, it said. See the World. Best Prices in Toronto.

Whatever Tammi did in there took about fifteen minutes. When she came out, she tucked an envelope into the carrying bag behind the stroller and turned back the way she came.

Waiting had given me time to work out a plan. I cut across the street again, opened the door and went inside.

Two guys about my age were slouched down in webbed plastic garden chairs, reading travel magazines. When I breezed in they checked me out in that sleazy way some guys do — eyes boring through my clothes from head to toe, with several stops in between. I ignored them. I was on a mission.

A counter ran across the back of the store, and the man behind it had deep lines between his nose and his mouth, and several more creasing his forehead. A forest of curly chest hair peeked out through the open neck of his shirt.

"What can I do for the pretty girl today?" he said. His smile was friendly, but he had wandering eyes too. The creeps out front were probably his kids.

I took a deep breath. Act, I told myself. Act your little heart out. "I was hoping you could help me," I said, flashing my best smile. "If you wouldn't mind answering some questions?"

A bead curtain hanging behind the counter flipped open and a tiny, very old woman bustled out. Her thin grey hair was pulled back into a knot and her jaw sunk into her neck as if she didn't have a tooth in her head. She was too old to be Trevor's wife, so she had to be his mother.

There was something tough about her, tough in a good way. She didn't say a word but she folded her skinny arms across her high little pot belly and glared at the two guys behind me, at Trevor, and at me.

"You from the government?" Trevor said.

"No, no. It's a project for my school. I have some questions about the travel business." I fished my history notebook out of my knapsack and opened it to a page with writing on it. Then I grabbed a pen. "Like, um, what country do most of your clients travel to?"

Trevor grinned. "That is easy question," he said. "They go home. To Philippines, to Somalia, to Croatia, to Serbia, to Vietnam. Where home is, they go."

I scribbled a few words in the margin of my book while I was planning the next question. "Are your clients mostly men or women?"

"Men," he said. "Few women also."

"And the men, do they buy tickets just for themselves, or do they take their families with them," I said.

"For self mostly. Sometimes for family," he said. "Sometimes is nice to escape wife." He smiled slyly.

The woman didn't like that at all. She flicked her eyes towards mine. Her words, in her own language, were as sharp as a cut across the mouth.

"There was a woman who left just before I got here," I said. "A woman with a baby. Did she buy a ticket just for herself, or what?" I tried out a sly sort of smile myself.

Trevor winked. "Pretty lady," he said. "She buys for self, for baby, for man. Maybe he is husband, maybe somebody else."

The old lady laughed at that, and just to be friendly, so did I.

"Well, I hope she's going somewhere nice," I said. "Someplace glamorous, like Paris or Venice or ..."

Trevor shrugged. "United States," he said. "Then maybe South America." He wiggled his hands up and down in front of him. "Maybe not."

CHAPTER 24

Flavia and Jon already knew that Raffi had been arrested, and that my dad was involved, but they didn't know about the new evidence. We met at my place and the three of us lounged around in our big front room while I brought them up to date. I told them about Tammi's planned trip with her boyfriend, about Al Green and Ray being the same person, about Ronny Roach being the second witness, and about Raffi's fingerprints being in Tammi's apartment.

"My dad said he'd talk to the police about the Roach," I said. "But we can't expect much to happen until Raffi's trial."

"You mean," Jon said, "that even though you can prove the Roach hates you, and probably lied about seeing Raffi just to get even with you, you can't do anything about it?"

"Not yet," I said. "Not until the Roach gives his story in court. Then, when the jury hears my side, hopefully they won't believe a word he says."

"Mr. Raffi must stay in jail?" Flavia asked.

I nodded. "Unless we can produce a miracle."

"I know something," Flavia said. "But it is not your miracle, Jess. Mrs. Tammi did not tell me of this trip, she told me she was moving to another apartment. I am feeling very suspicious about her."

"I wonder when she's going," I said. "I should probably tell my father." I got up from my chair. "Hey, who wants a Coke? It's Diet."

Flavia did, but Jon didn't. I handed her the can, opened mine, and set it on the floor beside my chair.

"Those fingerprints in Tammi's apartment are the real problem," I said. "I mean, there's two theories, right? The cops say Raffi was there, and his prints prove it. My theory is that somebody took a soft drink can and a magazine that he'd touched, and planted them there."

"But where would this person get such things?" Flavia said.

"It wouldn't be hard to scoop a soft drink can," Jon said. "I mean he could have just tossed it somewhere. The magazine would be harder to come by. What kind of magazine, do you know?"

I shrugged. Then I picked up my drink. Halfway to my mouth my hand stopped. Then I began to laugh.

Jon and Flavia looked at each other and shrugged. "She's losing it," Jon said. "This whole thing's been too much for her."

"Excuse me?" Flavia looked puzzled. "What is Jess losing?"

"Her mind."

"Ah," Flavia said. "Losing it."

By this time I was giggling hysterically, slapping the palms of my hands on my legs so hard they hurt.

"Jess!" Jon said. Then he grabbed my wrists and held them. "You really are losing it."

"It's just that," I said. "Just that..." I was almost sobbing by now. "I did it," I said. "I put those things in Tammi's apartment."

"But why?" Flavia said. "Why would you hurt Mr. Raffi?"

I pulled my wrists away from Jon. "I didn't mean to. Remember how I was babysitting for Brianna the night before the murder? Well, it was the same night really, the night Ray was killed. That was why the cops wanted to talk to me in the first place. You aren't going to believe this, but when I went down there I took a can of Diet Coke with me, because all Tammi ever has is ordinary Coke. And I took one of Mom's magazines. And I left it there, because Tammi wanted to borrow it. There was some article she wanted to read, about how to do your hair or something."

Jon was frowning. "So how did Raffi's prints..."

"He reads everything," I said. "Cereal boxes, flyers, everything. Cover to cover. So that's easy. And the Coke can, well..." I laughed again. "He put them in the fridge!"

"You aren't making sense, Jess," Jon said. "What did he put in, and in whose fridge?"

"Sorry," I said. "This is just so wild!" I made a big effort to pull myself together. "Raffi always puts the pop away. He carries it up the stairs, in cases. Then he sets them on the stove, slits the plastic covers with a knife, and puts a bunch of cans in the fridge. He does it the same way every time. So when I took one, he'd already handled it. So it would have his fingerprints on it, as well as mine."

"You must tell your father about this," Flavia said.

"Yes. The great thing is that Dad wasn't told what kind of pop can or what kind of magazine the prints were on, so when I identify them" I said, "maybe we can get Raffi released!"

"This whole thing is like a bad joke," Jon said. "Raffi..."

He said something else, but I was only half listening because I heard somebody on the stairs. At first I thought it was Mom, but Mom comes up at a run, and this person was walking. I got up and opened the door.

"Hi," Tammi said. "Can I borrow your phone? Mine's disconnected already because of the move and all, and there's nobody home at the Orellanas'." Then she noticed Jon and Flavia. The phone sat on a small table between them.

"You can use the extension in my room if you want," I said.

My eyes followed her down the hall. When she disappeared I whipped across the room, crouched in front of the answering machine, and pressed the *Record* button. As I straightened up, Tammi's voice bounced out at me. Jon's hand flew to the volume control. He turned it down so we couldn't hear anything. I looked at his eyes, then at Flavia's.

"Is this an awful thing to do?" I whispered. Neither of them answered. I grinned nervously. "I don't care," I said. "This is war."

Tammi didn't talk long. When she came back down the hall, I went with her to the door. "You're really moving?" I said.

She nodded. "Yeah. It spooks me, this place. Hey, say good-bye to your mom for me, will you? And ..." She didn't complete her sentence.

"And Raffi?" I said. I watched her to the first landing. When I came back into the room, Jon's finger was hovering over the *Play* button.

"Keep the sound low," I said.

The first voice on the tape was Tammi's, the second was a man's.

Hi, it's me.

You took your sweet time! I've been waiting here for an hour!

Sorry. The phone's disconnected. I wanted to call from the Orellanas' but they weren't home, so I had to come up to the Marchs'.

So?

I don't know. That Jess, she suspects something.

Don't be such a worry-wart. Everything's fine! Hey, did you get the tickets?

Yes. The train leaves at nine tonight, so meet me... how about in the line-up where you wait to board.

What gate?

I don't know. Do I have to do everything? It's the train to Chicago. Ask some-body.

OK, OK. How are you getting there? You taking a cab?

Yeah.

Jess isn't standing right there listening, is she? Tell me you're not that stupid.

I'm not that stupid. I'm in her room. The door's shut.

OK. I'll see you later. Don't mess up.

There were two clicks as two receivers were replaced. Jon pressed the *stop* button. He had no idea who that man was. Flavia didn't know either, I could tell to look at her.

I knew who he was. I recognized his voice. "Do you believe in ghosts?" I said.

CHAPTER 25

It took seventeen minutes to track down my father. Nobody answered at his office, and when I called his home, I got the kid.

"It's urgent," I said.

"Sorry. I can take a message. Who shall I say is calling?"

I groaned. "Jess March," I said.

"Hey, are you...?"

"Yeah," I said. "I am. Is your mother there?"

Speaking to my father's new wife wasn't something I was really wild about doing, but her kid was hopeless. When she came on the line, she sounded cagey, like she spent her life protecting my dad from people who were trying to bother him, me included. Maybe I was being unfair. Maybe he knew a lot of flakes. Still, she had to know I was his daughter. She could have said hello.

"I think I could possibly locate him," she said. "If it's really necessary, but ..."

"It's absolutely necessary," I said.

"Well, then, why don't I try to find him, and if I do, I'll have him call you."

I sighed. "What happens if you can't find him? When will he be home?"

"It could be late," she said. "After ten, at least. Are you sure this can't wait until tomorrow?"

"It can't wait. It's about a murderer," I said. "A murderer who's going to leave the country." Then I gave her my number.

It was five-thirty when Dad called. "Are you all right?" he said. "What's this about a murder? Not another one?"

"No," I said. "But I've figured out the one we've got." Then I told him about Tammi's call. I even played him the tape.

"You're sure about this, Jess?" he said, when it ended. "If you're right, we'll have to get the police down to the station to arrest him. If you're wrong, we're going to feel awfully stupid."

"I'm not wrong," I said. "Remember how you showed me the police report? Remember how the corpse didn't have red hair? The dead man wasn't Ray Bird, he was Al Green. They're two separate people. Ray Bird is the murderer. And he's alive and well and getting ready to split for Chicago. I'd know his voice anywhere."

"OK," Dad said. "I hope you realize that you're a key player in all this. You'll have to come to the station too."

"Me?" I said.

"Yes, you. You're the only one who can identify this Bird fellow. If we find him, he's going to deny being who he is, and I doubt we can count on his wife identifying him correctly."

"Hardly," I said. "Since she's already said he's dead."

"I'm going to be on the phone with the Crown Attorney and the police for a while so I don't think I'll have time to pick you up, but I'll meet you there. Can you take a cab..."

I laughed. "A cab to the station? Maybe I can share Tammi's."

"Poor idea," he said. "I'm glad you've still got your wits about you. What about the street-car? Have you got someone who can go with you. You shouldn't be out..."

"Alone at night," I said. Jon was pointing to Flavia and himself and nodding. "I have at least one friend who'll come. It's OK. Where do we meet?"

"Hmm," he said. "It's critical that the Birds don't see you. You know where the washrooms are on the departure floor?"

"I'll find them," I said.

"They're in the big waiting room that's separated off from the main part where the ticket counter is. Wait for me in the section directly across from the washrooms. It seems to me there are pillars there. If there are, get behind one."

"OK. What time?"

"If the train's at nine, people will be lining up long before that. Eight o'clock?"

"Sure."

"And Jess? Don't do anything heroic. That man is a killer."

I met Jon at his house shortly before seven.

"No Flavia?" he asked.

"Her mom didn't want her to come, because of the police being involved, but she lent me her jacket." I held up the shopping bag containing my disguise.

When I went into the Bells' downstairs washroom, I was myself: a teenager in jeans, T-shirt, and sandals. When I came out I was a sophisticated woman, one Tammi would never recognize, at least not at first glance. Flavia's black cotton blazer was a bit tight, but if I didn't do up the buttons I wouldn't split any seams. Underneath I had on a black T-shirt and stretchy black pants I borrowed from Mom. I'd also borrowed her white heels, some dangling silver ear-rings, a very red lipstick and a lacy white straw hat she'd never even worn yet.

Jon looked different too. His suit was pale grey, and it fit him perfectly. Under it he was wearing a white shirt with fat pink stripes. His tie was pink with huge orange flowers; it was so awful I couldn't take my eyes off it. He had a hat too, a cloth one with a stitched brim, the kind the ads say will still look good after you throw it over the side of your canoe.

Union Station is just a hop, skip and a jump from where the big highways streak along between the lake and the bottom of the city. The building is made of dull grey stone, and it takes up a whole block. That's on the street level, where you can see it. There's a lot more of it underneath because it's not only a train station, it's a subway stop and a commuter-train terminal as well.

Tammi would come in the main door on Front Street, where taxis let off their passengers. Jon and I transferred from the streetcar to the subway, so we arrived on the basement level. Then we worked our way up to the departure floor, which was difficult, because by this time I could hardly walk. The combination of no stockings, hot weather, sweaty feet, and too-small shoes was the perfect formula for a blister. It was a killer, the kind that pops its bubble almost immediately so the shoe gets to rub on the tender little circle of rawness underneath.

When we got to the waiting room where we were to meet my dad, Jon got me a hunk of toilet paper from the men's room and I made myself a little bandage. Then I stuck it between my shoe and my heel, and left a little flap hanging over the top. So much for sophistication.

We were waiting behind a pillar, exactly where Dad said we should be, by five to eight. He arrived at eight-twenty. He wasn't wearing his ordinary clothes either, at least not his lawyer clothes, which were all I'd seen him in for as long as I could remember. His jeans looked clean but old, his runners were that dingy grey colour white turns into, and his jean jacket had a torn cuff. He grinned when he saw me staring. "The real me," he said. Then he turned to Jon. "You must be Jess's friend. I'm Gordon March."

Jon, who had already jumped to his feet, introduced himself. Dad motioned him down again, then crouched in front of us. "Any sign of them?" he said.

I shook my head.

"What worries me is that our suspects will take one look at us and make a run for it. And then we're left with nothing. Nothing but Raffi in jail and a whole lot of egg on our faces."

There was something else to worry about too, but I didn't like to mention it. I was worried about being wrong. What if the man I'd heard on the phone wasn't Ray at all? I'd been pretty sure of myself at home. You could even say I was very sure of myself. Now that the cops were involved and they were depending on me being right, I wasn't sure about anything.

Dad looked at his watch. "Here's the plan," he said. "Two uniformed police officers are waiting in the first class lounge, which is just off the area by the gates. One of them is Sheena Bowes. She can identify Tammi Bird, so she'll already be watching her and anyone else with her. Does that sound OK so far?"

I nodded. "Yeah," I said.

"There are also two plainclothes cops somewhere in the vicinity. I'm not sure exactly where, but they know me, and they'll be following us or watching us the whole time. What we're going to do, the three of us, is walk past the people waiting to board the Chicago train. When we come to Mrs. Bird, and hopefully we will, I want you, Jess, to nudge me with your elbow, because otherwise I won't know we're close. OK?"

"Sure," I said.

"What you have to do then is get a good look at the guy with her. Good enough to identify him. You also have to let me know he's the right person, so I can then signal the cops. They won't move until I do that."

"I should say his name, or something?"

"His name would be great."

"What happens then?" Jon said.

"The cops will arrest him." Dad looked at his watch again. "Time to go. People will be boarding the train soon," he said. "We want to catch them before that."

"What if...?" I said.

Dad raised his eyebrows. "What if what?" he said.

"What if I can't identify him?"

"We all go home," he said. "And some of us feel stupider than others. Don't worry about it."

"Sure," I said. Then I stood, and winced.

"What's the matter?" Dad said. "Nerves?"

"A blister. It's nothing." Two lies, one after the other. My nerves were dancing, and the blister was agony. I shifted the toilet paper around in my shoe, but it didn't help. Dad looking at his watch again didn't help either. My whole leg felt like it was seeping out that one burning little hole, but I did what I had to do. I told myself how tough I was, and ignored it.

Dad took my arm on one side, and Jon walked beside me on the other, sort of brushing his hand against mine, like he was reminding me he was there. We passed through the main lobby where people get their tickets, and went down the ramp into the huge hall where they line up to board.

The departure gate for the Chicago train was at the far end, a city block away, a long block. The line-up straggled for half that distance. Suitcases and backpacks littered the floor on either side of it. The people were a real mixture; old people, middle-aged people, students. Some were really dressed up, others totally casual. Most of them were standing. A few sat on their luggage. One guy was reading a book, with one foot resting on his briefcase. There were kids all over the place. Kids in baby carriers, kids in strollers, kids pulling at their parents and squirming, kids whining. Everybody was waiting, and everybody was facing away from us.

As we reached the end of the line-up, I noticed that people were still joining it. I turned to Dad. "What if they come behind us?"

"When we get to the front we'll turn around and walk back," he said. "It would be best if you just looked for them, Jess. Fretting won't help." He sounded grumpy. He probably thought I was going to mess up and embarrass him.

Fretting might not help, but I was doing it anyway, because I didn't know which Tammi to look for. Would she be the old Tammi with the miniskirt and hair all over the place, or the new Tammi with the widow clothes and hair like Mom's? Every time I saw somebody the right size, who had a baby, I had to look at her really carefully.

Lots of women have that hair-all-over-the-place look. A couple even had dark roots and orange ends, just like Tammi. The first woman I picked out was too short; the second was pregnant.

As we got closer and closer to the front of the line, I started to panic. I had to find them. If I didn't, Raffi was going to stay in jail, my father was going to be embarrassed, Sheena was going to think I was playing games again, and my left foot was going to be mutilated for nothing.

I knew her immediately, even from behind. Part of her hair was pulled back with a big pink barrette, but the rest hung loose. She was wearing her purple miniskirt, a tight purple ribbed sweater, and high heels. Brianna, all in pink, was sleeping in the stroller. There was a man standing beside them. A tall, large man. I jerked my elbow into Dad.

The man was wearing a peaked baseball cap, and sunglasses. His hair was dark brown, not red, and for one awful minute I was convinced I'd been wrong. Then I moved up beside Tammi, and looked past her, right into Ray's face. "Hi," I said.

"Jess!" My name hissed out from between his teeth, just like it did that night in Brianna's room. I'd surprised him again. This time he wasn't laughing.

I knew the police were there, and my father was there, and Jon too, but I never felt so alone in all my life. My voice shook a little, but it was good and loud. "This man is Ray Bird," I said. "His hair is brown now, but that's just dye."

Dad's arm shot up into the air, like he was putting his hand up in school. At the same time, he was pushing me behind him. Then Sheena was there, and some other cops I didn't know, and Ray was running, running like a wild man towards the gate and the stairs to the train platform. The chain to keep the passengers back didn't stop him at all. He vaulted over it and passed the guard, who stepped backwards and flattened himself against the wall to get out of the way. All around me people were grabbing their kids and diving for cover. Sheena moved like the wind. When Ray was halfway up the stairs she was right there, at the bottom.

"Stop or I'll shoot," she yelled. Then she braced her feet and pointed her gun.

Ray kept going. When the single shot rang out, he staggered to the side of the stairs, balanced himself with one hand on the wall and raised the other above his head. A dark red stain seeped through his jeans, high on the outside of his thigh.

"She shot him!" Jon said. "He's bleeding! She didn't have to do that!"

"Yes, she did," I snapped. "She had to stop him."

Dad gave us both a hug. "Let's be calm here," he said. "It doesn't appear to be too serious, since he's still standing. It's probably just a flesh wound. Sensitive place, though," he added.

"A bummer," I said. "Has anybody seen Tammi?"

CHAPTER 26

The pay phone I was using was on the lower level of the station. I stood on one leg in front of it, pushing the buttons for Mom's work number, and admiring the mess that was my left heel. I'd called her from home, to tell her where I was going and what I was trying to do, but that was hours ago. By now she'd be having a haemorrhage.

She must have been sitting on the phone. "What happened?" she said.

"It *was* Ray. And they caught him."

"So he did it? He killed that other guy?" Then she started to cry. "And Raffi..., Raffi had nothing to do with it?"

"Raffi's innocent, Mom. The cops will have to let him go now, because the man he was supposed to have killed isn't dead — he's alive and *he's* the murderer. Anyhow all the evidence against Raffi was garbage. That's what Dad said."

"When? When can he come home? He doesn't even know all this has happened! He still thinks he's the major suspect! He's so depressed..."

"Tomorrow, probably. Dad said something about paperwork and the Crown Attorney and a judge. He told Sheena that Raffi shouldn't ever have been arrested because, get this, a kid could figure out what happened." I laughed. "So he thinks she'll hurry things up. Anyhow, he's going to see Raffi tonight, to tell him the good news."

Mom didn't say anything for a bit, but I could almost hear her thinking. "You did it, Jess. Didn't you? Ray would have got away if it wasn't for you."

"I guess," I said. "And Dad."

"Tell him thanks," she said. "From me."

◆◆◆

"Mom says thanks," I said. "She was really happy."

"Nice to have something work out so well," Dad said. He and Jon and I were sitting in the back part of the Station Restaurant, shoving the food in like we hadn't eaten in a week. Burgers, fries, rings and shakes. A fat fix.

"I've asked Sheena to join us," Dad said. "We need to clear up some details."

There were a lot of cops around now. Two of them even checked out the restaurant while we were sitting there. They were looking for Tammi, asking every woman with a baby to show identification.

I watched them. "They're not going to find her," I said.

Dad reached across me for the vinegar. "It would be good if they do. That was quite a story she told, pretending the dead man, Al Green, was her husband."

"You think she could go to jail for that?" Jon said.

Dad moved his hand palm up, palm down a couple of times. "If they don't find her, she'll be a running for the rest of her life, waiting to be arrested. If they find her now, everything will be dealt with, and it will be all over. She'd probably just get a slap on the wrist."

"Why?" Jon said. "She caused a heap of trouble."

Dad finished his fries and started stealing mine. "Ah, her husband made her do it," he said. "That's pretty obvious from what Jess said. Remember, Jess? You said Tammi cried for hours the night of the murder."

"I thought she cried because Ray was dead, but I guess not," I said. "You think he made her do that? Say the body was him?"

"Don't you?" Dad asked.

Sheena set her tray in the empty space beside Jon, and sat down. "It really busts me up to have to shoot somebody. And the more bust up I get, the hungrier I am," she said. Her tray was loaded.

"Good shot," Dad said.

"Yeah, it was, wasn't it?" She unwrapped her first hamburger, lifted the top piece of bun, and held it in the air. "Tricky when he was hoofing it up the stairs like that." She winked. "Gave him a little something to remember me by, didn't I? A little dimple in his right cheek. Can somebody pass the ketchup?"

"No sign of Mrs. Bird?" Dad asked.

Sheena's hamburger hovered near her mouth. "She must have cut out during all the excitement. We shoulda had somebody watching her, but to tell the truth..." She looked at me, and shook her head. "We thought Jess was just being creative again."

Dad looked puzzled. "Again?"

"It's a long story," I said.

Sheena's mouth was full, so we watched her until she finished chewing. "You did good work, Jess. What really burns me is that none of us clued in about the corpse not being Bird."

Dad offered me the last of my fries. I took it. "Everybody makes mistakes," he said.

"Shouldn't have happened." Sheena shook her head in disgust. "Sure we had the grieving widow, but when we printed the body and found out he was really Al Green, we should of figured it out."

"Any idea what the connection was between Bird and this Green fellow?" Dad said.

"Well, Green robbed a bank, we know that. We also know he had a partner who never got caught, a partner who took off with the money. Green got a jail term, and I guess Bird, the partner, got the loot. That's the way I figure it anyway," Sheena said.

"So when Green was released, he came looking for his old buddy," Dad said. "I guess it wasn't a terrific reunion."

"I've got a question," Jon said. "What's going to happen to Ronny Roach?"

"What do you mean?" Sheena said. "Why should something happen to him? You think he got a little creative too?"

I sighed. I just wanted the Roach to go away. Far away.

"Don't tell me we messed that up too," she said.

I sighed again. "It wasn't your fault," I said. Then I looked at Jon, and Dad. "Could you tell her?" I said. "I don't even want to talk about him."

They did. Jon told most of it.

"I knew Jess was having troubles, but I never knew who he was," Sheena said.

I shook my head. "I should have told you."

"Well, I'll have to follow up on that. We can't have people misleading the police and get away with it. Mr. Roach and I will definitely have to have a little discussion. At the police station."

"Misleading the police," I said. "Now where have I heard that before?"

Dad frowned. "Have I missed something here? This conversation seems to be going on on two levels. One I understand, and one I don't."

"Not to worry, Mr. March." Sheena said. "Jess here got a little protective about Raffi early on. Caused a bit of confusion. No big deal. Not now."

The party started out kind of small: Mom and Raffi; Jon and me; the Orellana family; Kelly and Joey; and a few of Raffi's friends. As evening came and it got darker and the stars came out, we spread from the apartment to the back deck, then down to the back yard, out to the front yard, and across the street to Raffi's building. What we ended up with was almost a block party. People just kept coming, partly because everybody likes Raffi, and partly because of the three guys playing steel drums.

I'd asked Dad, but I didn't really expect him so it was a nice surprise when he showed up. I was glad he did. For one thing, I liked his wife a lot better in person than I did on the phone. Her kid was something else. A smart-mouth thirteen-year-old. Just what I need in my life.

The worst thing that happened, and the silliest, was when Mom and Dad ended up about a foot away from each other, back to back on the front sidewalk. When they turned around at the same time and saw they were almost rubbing noses, they both stepped backwards. It was funny I guess, but sad too. You could tell they felt dumb about avoiding each other, so they sort of pressed their cheeks together, or almost together. Mom was a little stiff and Dad got stupidly jolly, but they were OK.

The best part was when Dad fell in love with Raffi's portrait of me. That was important, because Raffi didn't want to take charity, so he needed to pay Dad. Dad, who knew how poor Raffi was, and who wanted to be a nice guy because of me, kept saying there was no charge, and he hadn't really done much anyway. What the portrait did was give them a way to work that out. Raffi offered to do a new one of me for Dad's office. So Dad was happy, and Raffi was happy. The only one who wasn't too happy was Mom, and that had nothing to do with the portrait, it had to do with something Dad said.

"Paint her in that lacy white straw hat," he told Raffi. Then he turned to me. "You know Jess, the one you wore at the station. You looked smashing in it, just smashing. I guess you can leave off your mom's shoes though."

"My new white hat?" Mom said. "My good summer shoes?" Her hands were on her hips and she wasn't smiling. Wearing her clothes is one of those things that's a complete no-no, even if I ask first.

"Oh, shoot," I said.

RIVER WEST SCHOOL
LIBRARY